This Is Not Who We Are

To Victoria and to my son Théo

This Is Not Who We Are

Sophie Buchaillard

Seren is the book imprint of
Poetry Wales Press Ltd.
Suite 6, 4 Derwen Road, Bridgend, Wales, CF31 1LH
www.serenbooks.com
facebook.com/SerenBooks
twitter@SerenBooks

The right of Sophie Buchaillard to be identified as
the author of this work has been asserted in accordance
with the Copyright, Designs and Patents Act, 1988.

© Sophie Buchaillard, 2022

ISBN: 9781781726648
Ebook: 9781781726655

The publisher acknowledges the financial assistance of the Books Council
of Wales.

Printed in Bembo by Severn, Gloucester.

This Is Not Who We Are

A genocide is the systematic killing of a large
group of people based on
someone else's criteria of otherness.

'From what I gather from those who have studied the
history of genocide – its definition and application – there
seems to be a pattern.'
(Toni Morrison, in *Mouth Full of Blood*)

Foreword

In April 1994, the plane of the President of Rwanda was shot down over Kigali. His murder sparked a mass extermination of the Tutsi population and any Hutu who supported them which lasted 100 days, led to the gruesome death of over 800,000 people, and was systematically ignored by the West. I was sixteen years old at the time and for a few months in 1994, I corresponded with Victoria, a girl my age who had fled Rwanda for the refugee camp of Goma, in neighbouring Zaïre. One day she wrote that she was being moved. After that, her letters stopped. I never found out what happened to her. A man involved in the French response told me nothing could be done. I believed him. He was my father.

Iris

As a child, washing machines fascinated me. I would sit in front of the circular glass, watching water swooshing around into a whirlpool of colourful clothing. Bubbles would form against the hard surface, instantly swept away by the next revolution of the drum. Purring, rocking the dirt away, until clothes came out of their womb – warm, safe, unblemished.

Now, my thoughts were less soothing. If humanity could crawl into such a device, could we erase the indelible marks which stain us? Incomprehensible threads kept pouring into my mind. The lack of sleep wasn't helping. Still, evenings were our special time and this one was no different. After the bath, I wrapped Ophelia into a sleepsuit, nestled her on my chest and rocked her to sleep with a story from my childhood. One of her favourites, a tale of the birth of Rwanda, the Mwami and his three sons. Afterwards, I placed her in the cot, under the watchful eye of her favourite Rabbit. I held her hand, not quite ready to let go, knowing that in only a few days she would be starting nursery, and I would cease to be the sum of her world.

'We recommend parents bring their children for a settling-in day before they start with us,' the nursery manager explained over the phone. 'Our days are broken into thirty-minute periods. We alternate the type of activities to stimulate your child's development and build in regular breaks so as not to overwhelm them.' So many details. This woman was used to dealing with anxious parents keen to mitigate their sense of guilt with a barrage of zealous enquiries. 'Of course, all our nursery nurses are fully qualified. A certificate in childcare is essential to become part of the Rainbow Oak family.' She sounded like an infomercial.

'Very impressive,' I replied, repressing the urge to scream. 'Ophelia and I will see you tomorrow then,' I managed before putting the phone down.

After seven months on maternity leave, my body had acquired a doughy consistency. I lived wrapped in misshapen leggings and t-shirts stolen from Henry's weekend pile. I felt starved, hungry to plunge my teeth into a new project. It wasn't the solitude. Like all writers, I thrived on absence. It was more as if mother and writer had been battling for supremacy over my mind, and the writer was losing. The niggling voice was growing louder: what if? What if the lack of sleep had annihilated my intellectual abilities? I had hardly stretched past decisions about whether to crush a banana or boil a sweet potato since Ophelia was born. What if I had forgotten how to write? I had assumed I would have plenty of time to write whilst 'the baby' was asleep. As soon as Ophelia started her nap, I transformed into this...*thing*: I swirled around the kitchen, piling dirty dishes in the sink, putting reusable nappies and sleepsuits in the washing machine, stacking plastic toys back into their boxes, feverish with a sudden need to bring back order to the little one-bedroom flat that marked the boundaries of our realm. Only the modulating cry emanating from Ophelia's bedroom would pull me out of this frenzy, grounded by the need to change her nappy. In this bizarre realm, words were superfluous. The rhythm of our lives was dictated by her cries, and the cycle of the washing machine. It was doubt which had pushed me to reach for the phone, finding the closest community nursery that would take her. They would take her.

The next day, I dropped Ophelia on the doorstep of Rainbow Oak Nursery, where a rotund nursery nurse took charge. 'We'll keep her in until midday,' she said. 'I'll ring you immediately if she gets distressed.' The woman was stout, probably in her late sixties. The Rainbow Oak Nursery logo protruded from her airbag-like bosom. I bet she gives amazing hugs, I thought, envious. 'Right, I'd better go then. I can see Ophelia is in excellent hands.'

On my own for the first time in seven months, I marched to the nearest coffee house, ordered a latte, claimed an isolated spot, and unwrapped the cellophane from a new notebook. This was it. The moment of truth. At first, I thought my mind was blank. Once I had phased out the ambient noise, all I could think about was my childhood. You've got to start somewhere, Iris, I told myself.

The school I attended in France had doubled as a convent for a handful of Assumptionist nuns – kind, elderly women dressed in pale grey habits and wrapped in woolly cardigans of neutral colours, well suited to their kind nature. They still wore the veil in those days, so we could only guess at the short crop of white hair underneath. They were a disappearing tribe, even then.

The convent in its heyday had housed up to thirty nuns and as many novices, but cloistered life had been decimated by the temptations of modernity. In my time at the school, there were only four left: one Mother Superior who doubled as the head teacher; two sisters, one who (incongruously I thought) taught biology, the other who was custodian of our history lessons. The last one, Sister Agnes, was a nun-in-training. She did not wear the veil, and often didn't wear the habit either, partial to baggy jeans and chunky knitwear instead. The sisters seemed unsure what to do with this young girl and her thick wavy curls; so long had it been since their own vows. She had been put in charge of gymnastics – on account of her youth rather than any sporting abilities. She also helped with the choir and catechism. I often wondered what the sisters had been thinking, leaving us unsupervised with this exalted character – you would have had to be exalted to want to take your vows in the 1990s. And indeed, nothing seemed to ever dampen her spirit. Strangely, I don't remember her face. Only the woollen clothing she wore, because they made her at odds with the formality of the sisters, more one of us.

It would have been Wednesday, since we were in catechism. The lesson had just ended. Sister Agnès had moved on to the weekly announcements. The priest needed a volunteer to help with flower arrangements in the chapel; the Parent Association was organising a bake sale to raise money for the Order's project in Eastern Africa; next week's lesson would be on Corinthians 13: 4-13.

The bell rang, calling us to the next class. 'Oh, and one other thing. I'm looking for volunteers to become penfriends with girls in one of our missions. Anyone interested?' We looked at each other, daring someone to raise their hand. 'No one wants an African correspondent?' She seemed to look straight at me as she said it. I liked her; I wanted her to be pleased with me somehow. I raised my hand, 'Yeah, I'll do it.'

She smiled, wrote my name down in her little notebook. 'Good,' she said, 'come to my office later.'

After class, I made my way to the minuscule office in the school basement, next to the boiler room. A storeroom for forgotten things. I had heard rumours about the Germans occupying the building during the war. Music echoing through the basement made me pause. I imagined the laughter of soldiers entwined with the crystalline voices of their female companions. Favour-seekers. Lovers. Survivors. Women, soon to be shaven. A gesture intended to shame. To erase the past.

As I stepped into the room, the music stopped.

'Come in,' she called. 'I was planning the school concert.'

The room was small and stuffy, the air kept humid by the monstrous boiler. Beads of sweat collected on my upper lip, clinging to fine hairs.

'The heat's playing havoc with my guitar,' she said, pointing at the acoustic instrument resting against the wall. Staring at the music sheets scattered over the floor, I mopped the perspiration off my brow with the back of my hand, feeling my cheeks flashing red.

'So, have you had a penfriend before?'

The closest I had come was the girl from Touary. The school had arranged an exchange programme, a misguided attempt to sensitise us, city kids, to country living. The girl's parents raised pigs. They had invited the whole class to visit. A boy from the school had fallen into the cesspit, putting an end to the experiment, and his reputation. Not something I wanted to expand upon.

Distracted, Sister Agnès started scouring her desk, knocking piles of tapes that tumbled over stacks of loose papers.

'Here it is,' she said, brandishing a crumpled envelope stained with coffee rings. *Mission Assomptioniste camp de Goma* read the blue lettering on the top left corner. 'Any questions?'

I shook my head no, picked up the envelope and reversed into the corridor.

'Bring me your reply when it's ready. I'll arrange to have it sent,' she called after me.

The cool air from the staircase hit me, sending a shiver between my shoulder blades. Quickening my pace, I reached the stairs which I climbed two at a time. At the top, I pushed the rotating door, surfacing onto the familiar street.

My walk home retraced the memorable wide avenues tourists usually associated with Paris. Looking at the majestic white stone buildings, it was hard to imagine they had been engineered by Haussmann to curb civil unrest. The only clue was maybe the contrasting black wrought-iron doors and elaborate supporting caryatids spying over the unsuspecting passers-by. Many buildings in this part of the city were adorned with emblazoned flags like colourful elements of the nations they represented, signalling foreign embassies.

As I reached the Esplanade des Droits de L'Homme, I slowed my pace to manoeuvre around a swarm of tourists hoping for a shot of the Eiffel Tower. We had just finished the Second World War in history. I smiled at the thought that all those people had travelled to take a picture of what was little more than an oversized lightning rod, oblivious to the fact they stood on the site of the signature of the Universal Declaration of Human Rights. Still, France was known internationally for this towering symbol of industrial advance, rather than the less visible advance in codifying our civil legislation. Only a discreet bronze plaque read: *All men are born and remain free and equal in rights* – the first article of the Declaration of Human Rights. Crossing the square, I passed the stone statue of Benjamin Franklin. From his stately chair, he presided over the residential quarter of my childhood. A safe haven of propriety, steeped in wealth, old and new.

From the front door, I was drawn to the kitchen by the hum of the washing machine. Stretching my neck, I scanned the kitchen for signs of my mother. No pot cooking on the hob. No vegetables half peeled on the counter. No shopping bags balanced on the little table. Glad to discover I was the first one home, I set up the dinner table for three, poured myself a glass of milk and retreated to my room to open the letter. It was short and formal, written in crayon:

My name is Victoria Uwamahoro. I am from Rwanda but at the moment I am staying with the sisters in Zaïre. The sisters are very nice to us. They teach us. They say we can write, so I can practice my French. I want to become a translator, you see. I speak Kinyarwanda, French, and English.

Taking a sheet of paper out of my desk and a turquoise fountain pen, I replied, giving Victoria my name; offering a concise description of my family; asking whether she had brothers or sisters. It was a good place to start, I thought.

The answer took a few weeks to arrive.

I have two brothers. They are in the camp with me. We were separated from our parents on the way here. The sisters are helping us to locate them.

After that, we exchanged pictures – hers drawn with wax crayons on tracing paper, torn from school notebooks; mine on pristine white paper liberated from my father's printer. Victoria's letters arrived stamped and posted to my home address, causing a wave of excitement as I unsealed the next instalment in our exchange. We had learnt about each other in the peculiar way only correspondence allows. Each letter brought new crumbs: who she was. What she wanted to be. Carefully crafted words which sculpted the image she chose to project of herself. Her experience of life in the camp was treated as no more than an anomaly, almost as if it was tangential to our exchange rather than what had brought us together.

At school, the noviciate would add my letter to a pile of similar missives from the sisters, destined for Goma. I thought the nuns must have had a sort of clandestine postal service to provide the traumatised children with the illusion of normality. I had visions of letters hidden in missionary knickers, flown in with bags of rice and furtively tucked into schoolbooks. At the same time, I imagined the nuns in Goma like the ones in my school, in their pale grey habits, teaching swarms of children neatly seated behind little wooden tables. In my mind, it was dry and sunny, and the children were smiling.

Where did all that come from? I wondered, putting the pen down. I hadn't thought about Victoria in decades. I looked at my watch. It was time to collect Ophelia. I packed my things and got under way. The next day, I abandoned the leggings for something more civilised, dropped Ophelia off at nursery, and returned to the anonymity of the coffee house, eager to write.

The 10th of April 1994 was a Saturday. Like every Saturday, my parents and I had driven to the Latin Quarter for a ham and cheese crêpe, before going to the independent MK2 cinema in the Odeon. We had queued under the watchful eye of Danton's statue, undeterred by the coat of bird droppings that draped his revolutionary shoulders. I don't remember the film, just the moment when my father's pager vibrated. He picked up the little black box with its rectangular window glowing green, looked at the flashing code only he understood, sighed, stood up and left. My mum and I continued to watch. He was 'on call'. Outside the cinema, the front page of every paper spread across the green art deco kiosk of the newsagent showed the same story: the plane of the Rwandan President, Juvénal Habyarimana, had been shot down above Kigali airport two days before. Within minutes, roadblocks were put in place and Tutsi across the country were hunted and killed by the government soldiers and Interahamwe militia.

I pressed my thumb hard onto the neck of the pen, daydreaming. I had never visited Rwanda. I knew as much as anyone, which was pretty much nothing. I would need to do some research.

In the 1990s, Europe pictured Africa as this homogeneous blur with patches of desert and poverty – pot-bellied children with disproportionately large heads, swarms of black flies circling gunky eyes in sunken sockets. Africa was a place where bloody civil wars erupted like wildfires. Somalia was fresh in every memory.

Few people could have placed Rwanda on a map. Even fewer knew that the country was surrounded by African Great Lakes bearing the names of Rudolf, Edward, Albert, Victoria. On the border between Rwanda and Zaïre (now the Democratic Republic of Congo), there was another lake, Lake Kivu, near the town of Goma. In subsequent years, the British would blame the Hutu. Some French still blame the Tutsi.

Ophelia had adapted well to nursery. I suggested we extend to five days a week. It was good for her socialisation, I told Henry, who nodded, recognising the intense look in my eyes. He knew I had found a new writing project. The next day, I went to the library and borrowed everything I could find on Rwanda. I procured commission reports, journalistic accounts, testimonials from survivors on both sides. I was surprised by how much the narrative of the conflict shifted depending on whether the document was in French or in English; written by a UN rapporteur or a British journalist; witnessed by a Hutu civil servant or a Tutsi in exile. Books, articles, commission reports piled on my desk at home;

post-it notes with quotes scribbled for their significance. I cried as I read in an Agence France-Presse report that between April and July 1994, a million Tutsi were massacred with machetes. Wives and daughters raped. Unborn children carved out of their mother's belly. Corpses with missing limbs found in churches, scattered in gardens, thrown in large mass graves, discarded on the side of the road. One hundred days. It was hard to understand what could have led a people to turn on itself in this way. A Humanitarian Rights Watch report pointed at an administrative exercise built on racist premises. I wondered how a political minority could have manipulated an entire country into committing mass genocide.

I kept coming back to my father's pager lighting up the cinema. He was working as a Special Advisor to the Ministry of Cooperation, an offshoot of Foreign Affairs that specialised in francophone areas of influence in Africa and Asia. It meant the French government knew. Immediately, they knew. And if they knew, did that mean the genocide had in fact been preventable?

By July, the advance of the rebel army, marching from Burundi to stop the genocide, had forced the mass exodus of the Hutu towards the border with Zaïre, to a place between lake Kivu and the town of Goma. Millions set up camp there, amongst them Victoria and her brothers. Goma – the place from where the blue letters had come. I found pictures of the camp, makeshift structures and NGO white tents, dishevelled women carrying water in plastic containers, piles of corpses mounting on the side of the road. I started having nightmares, lost my appetite. I wondered why Victoria had chosen not to mention the million who lost their lives to cholera and dysentery. Maybe with our letters she was clinging on to a last shred of humanity as the

French Army facilitated the retreat of the perpetrators. Amongst the chaos, she had chosen a narrative of hope.

Distortion was at the root of Rwanda's atrocities, I realised, which made Victoria's choice all the more brave. Words had been used to dehumanise people since before she was born. I learnt that historically the population of Rwanda was formed of a single people sharing one language – Kinyarwanda, one religion and one land. Traditionally, the term Tutsi had referred to those rich with cattle, whilst the Hutu were their serfs and the Twa were hunter-gatherers. This meant that siblings could be in different social classes, one being a Tutsi, another one a Hutu. I realised that I didn't know which Victoria and her brothers were, and maybe it was better that way. It angered me to discover it was the Belgians who had introduced an ethnic dimension. A narrative of hate had done the rest. By the time Rwanda claimed its independence, Tutsi had become *Inyenzi* (cockroaches), whilst Hutu called themselves *Interahamwe* (those with a single purpose or literally: 'those attacking together').

From the summer of 1994, I remembered little more than threads, incoherent details, memories of colourful words on tracing paper, vague news reports about human savagery, the green light of a pager. Dad was absent for three weeks, I remembered that. On his return, he had said something about a crisis cell. Now I was reading that French policy at the time had been decided by President Mitterrand, advised by an unelected unit headed by his own son. His own son, I thought. What I read next gave me a chill. The unit included staff from my father's Ministry. He worked in Co-operation, a special advisor to the Minister. I deduced that because of his role he would have seen the information coming in. Would have been behind the closed doors where decisions were made.

The more I thought about it, the less I was able to reconcile the loving father who meant the world to me with the grey-suited men who had contributed to the death of 800,000 human beings. I told myself he must have been misinformed somehow. After all, he had never set foot in Rwanda. Maybe that made it worse though, that men like him, with no real understanding of a situation thousands of kilometres away, could have the power to weigh into a conflict like that. I felt real rage at their arrogance, playing with human lives as if they were pawns on a chess board, whilst on the news, organised genocide was wilfully misrepresented as a spontaneous civil war between two ethnic groups. It was shoddy journalism. It was a crime against humanity. And my father – how could such a measured and kind man have been party to all this? I felt a sense of overwhelming shame for the casual missives I had sent Victoria as the enormity of what I had discovered slowly settled around me like so much debris after a plane crash. At home, it became difficult to make eye contact with Henry, as if to do so would reveal to him how messed up everything was inside my head. I hid in Ophelia's room at night, pretending to be telling her stories. I sat in the dark whilst she slept, lost under a pile of questions with no easy answers.

There was much discussion about authors appropriating the experience of others, as if to do so was to perpetrate yet another crime against the victims. Narrowly speaking, the victims were those who had been injured or destroyed by the genocide – the Tutsi and their sympathisers. In the camps, Hutu had suffered too. Died too. Then there was the broader idea that a victim ought to be anyone who had somehow been tricked or duped. This would include all the people of Rwanda who were manipulated by their own government; spectators in the West misled by poor reporting; citizens whose government knew and did nothing. Or, in the case of France, did too much. Did I have the agency to write about horrors my own country bore responsibility for? Was it some sort of sick voyeurism? Collective responsibility had proven a powerful solvent, erasing the stains of the individual. Collective guilt: if nobody is responsible, then everybody is responsible. Someone had said that. Maybe it was Pope Francis, talking about the abuse the Catholic church had committed against children. It seemed fitting. The Church had its share of responsibility in Rwanda too. They supported the Hutu Power movement.

I was at university in Bordeaux when the trial of Maurice Papon was taking place. A French civil servant during the Second World War, he had participated in the deportation of more than 1,600 Jews. The Germans had asked for adults; he had taken it upon himself to send the children too. As students, we had attended the trial, allegedly to watch justice being served. In truth, to catch a glimpse of a real-life monster. What we saw was an ordinary old man, a decorated civil servant at the end of a prolific career. He was convicted in 1998 at the age of eighty-eight, and served three years before being released on the grounds of ill health.

We were children when we corresponded, Victoria and I. But I never sought her out. I could have rung one of the charities seeking to track down survivors. I never did. I could have travelled there. I never wanted to. I felt awful about not asking her questions at the time. I watched the news with my parents, but it was as if the TV screens acted as filters obfuscating the truth. Like everyone else, I refused to see, and without witnesses, horror was allowed to fester.

When I thought about Victoria now, I felt like a grieving mother. Yet, there was an inherent contradiction in the idea of grieving when not knowing. To grieve was to abandon hope, admit defeat, let go. I had never found out who had moved

21

Victoria. Whether she had remained with her siblings. Who were the men (in my mind they must have been soldiers) who took her? I had wondered whether they wore the colourful shirts of the Hutu Power, the uniforms of the Rwandan Patriotic Army rebels; whether they were part of the Presidential Guard or the Rwandan Army. Not the blue helmets of the United Nations Assistance Mission for Rwanda, since they had left already. Maybe the heavily armed French soldiers who replaced them to the sound of *Vive la France.* Responsibility was never apportioned. I realised I might never find answers. But I could write. For a brief instant, in the summer of 1994, Victoria had lent me her scattered words, like pebbles on a foreign beach, so that one day I could find my way back to her.

Victoria

Mama and Data believed in the magic of names. They called me Victoria, after the great English Queen, to will my life full of successes. That was my first name. It was a heavy name which Mama's tongue always carried whole, proudly. Data too refused to cut it short. A name destined for greatness. On my identity card, it says another name. A much smaller name.

'Breakfast's ready,' Mama calls from the kitchen. My brothers and I find her swaying to the joyous music of her little transistor radio. Mama is about two things. Dancing and praying. Preferably together.

'Come on *abana*,' she urges.

Data says grace, then we eat.

'*Ibi biryo ni byiza*, Mama,' Data says. Mama's food is always good. She says it is because it is full of love.

At home, we speak Kinyarwanda. Outside the house we speak French. It is the language in which Data conducts business and the language of the Church. I love our many languages. So much more to say.

'Benjamin, Paul, *abahungu*, let's go!' I call to my brothers. I don't want to be late. Archbishop Vincent is visiting our church from St Michael's Cathedral today. Without waiting for Mama and Data, the boys and I burst out of the front door, pretending to dribble an imaginary ball along the street, all the way to the church in Gikondo.

The boys are faster. They are already inside when I reach the familiar brick-walled building capped with roof tiles so blue they make me think of Paradise. The Palatine community has decorated the entrance with flowers today, to celebrate Archbishop Vincent's visit. Father Peter is at the pulpit, welcoming us all.

'That's it, sister.' He waves at me to come to the front, 'There's room for everyone.'

I spot the boys, a few steps away. Paul is small and compact, dressed in a white shirt and red brick shorts. Benjamin is three heads taller, his shoulders wide and sturdy. I take my place amongst them, cross-legged on the dirt floor. Paul climbs into my lap. Seeing this, Benjamin smiles at his little brother and wraps a protective arm around me. We are blessed, I think.

Father Peter starts.

'Welcome, my children. Join me to welcome Monseigneur Archbishop Vincent.'

The choir starts singing in French. Soon, the boys are swaying next to me, hands clapping. I imagine this is what it must be like to meet a rock star. When the sound dies down, Father Peter intones the first reading. 'A reading from the Acts of the Apostles,' his voice thunders above our heads.

'It was about this time that King Herod started persecuting certain members of the church. He had James the brother of John beheaded, and when he saw that this pleased the Jews he went on to arrest Peter as well. As it was during the days of Unleavened Bread that he had arrested him, he put him in prison, assigning four sections of four soldiers each to guard him, meaning to try him in public after the Passover. All the time Peter was under guard the church prayed to God for him unremittingly. On the night before Herod was to try him, Peter was sleeping between two soldiers, fastened with two chains, while guards kept watch at the

main entrance to the prison. Then suddenly an angel of the Lord stood there, and the cell was filled with light. He tapped Peter on the side and woke him. 'Get up!' he said, 'Hurry!' – and the chains fell from his hands. The angel then said, 'Put on your belt and sandals.' After he had done this, the angel next said, 'Wrap your cloak round you and follow me.' He followed him out, but had no idea that what the angel did was all happening in reality; he thought he was seeing a vision. They passed through the first guard post and then the second and reached the iron gate leading to the city. This opened of its own accord; they went through it and had walked the whole length of one street when suddenly the angel left him. It was only then that Peter came to himself. And he said, 'Now I know it is all true. The Lord really did send his angel and save me from Herod and from all that the Jewish people were expecting.'

'This is the word of the Lord,' he concludes.

'Amen,' we repeat in chorus.

Father Peter's voice comes in and out of focus in the heat of the overcrowded church.

'As for me, my life is already being poured away as a libation, and the time has come for me to be gone…But the Lord stood by me and gave me power, so that through me the whole message might be proclaimed for all the pagans to hear; and so I was rescued from the lion's mouth. The Lord will rescue me from all evil attempts on me, and bring me safely to his heavenly kingdom…'

The archbishop's high-pitched voice breaks my torpor. I must have missed his reading of the Gospel. Now he is talking about the suffering of our people under Tutsi control; about the God-given power rising in our community. Next to me, Benjamin is drinking his words, captivated. Paul has lost interest and his observing a minuscule ant running along the side of his foot.

Back at the house that evening, Benjamin tells Mama and Data about Archbishop Vincent's message. *'Soyez fier, mes enfants. That's what he told us.'*

Data frowns. 'Pride is a sin, son.'

Mama crosses herself, looking away.

My brothers and I go to a religious school in a red brick building. Our classroom is a single square with whitewashed walls, rows and rows of individual wooden tables and cold metal chairs arranged side-by-side to face a huge blackboard where the sister writes our Theme of the Day. Today, she has written My Future with coloured chalks. Her face is soft and always full of smiles. Standing in front of the blackboard in her freshly pressed habits, she looks like an angel. She goes around the room, asking each of us what we want to be when we grow up. A truck driver. A teacher. A mother. It is my turn to speak.

'A translator,' I say.

A boy behind me laughs.

'Translators help us make sense of a bigger world,' she replies with an encouraging smile. She moves to the next child. A soldier, he says.

Through the white barred windows an explosion of voices interrupts the lesson. Another class, invading the playground to the sound of youthful excitement. For the next thirty minutes, they will run wild, chasing balls on the red earth. Inside, it is Celine's turn to speak. Celine is my best friend. Ignoring the colourful Future on the board, she asks about the green plaque outside our classroom. The plaque that says: *This building is a gift from the Belgian Mission.* My parents say that Rwandan girls are better seen than heard, but Celine is brave, always asking questions. The sister nods. Turning towards the rest of the class, she launches into an explanation about the chemical oxidation of copper. 'It turns cooking pots poisonous,' she adds, proud to have displayed her knowledge of chemistry. One of the boys near the door starts wriggling on his chair as if possessed, dropping off his chair onto the ground. The rest of the class explodes with wild giggles at the performance.

'Enough!' the sister bellows, bringing the class to order. Before Celine can ask another question, the sister has moved from her to the next child. Celine frowns.

'I wanted to know what the gift was for,' she whispers in my ear.

At break time, Celine and I always sit under a large tree a little distance away. From there we can observe the others playing games like through a television set. This is where I find Celine, red-eyed, snot glistening on her upper lip.

'Celine, are you OK? Did you hurt yourself?' She shakes her head, pulling her knees under her chin in a movement that reminds me of a threatened pangolin rolling into its carapace. I sit on the ground next to her, leaning against her, shoulder to shoulder. 'Go on, you can tell me,' I say.

Celine is silent for a long time, apart from the sobs that interrupt her breathing. I place the flat of my hand against her back, rubbing gently like Mama does, brushing the sorrow away.

'Does it matter?' she asks.

'Does what matter, Celine?'

'That I am, you know, a Tutsi – *inyenzi.*'

On hearing the word, I jerk backward. 'Who called you a cockroach?'

'It doesn't matter.'

'It does matter. Who, Celine?'

She whispers a name into my ear, my brother's name.

'Come with me,' I order, standing up.

I march towards the red building, Celine following a few steps behind. It is still breaktime and the sister is not back in the classroom yet. The older boys are sitting in a circle around a little transistor radio, listening to a voice filled with vehemence. They turn towards Celine, standing behind me like a shadow.

'Hutu Power,' the voice on the radio calls.

'Hutu Power,' the boys answer, as if in a trance.

The chilling fervour makes me take a step back; even my dear Benjamin has spoken the hateful words. Celine pulls at my sleeve, her shudder reaching me through my school uniform.

After class I walk Celine home in silence.

'Thank you,' she says before stepping across the threshold.

'For what?' I ask brusquely. 'I didn't do anything.'

'For being my friend.'

Back at our house, I wait until the boys have gone to bed. I find Data in the garden. I tell him what happened.

'There was real hatred in their eyes, Data. It scared me. Was I a coward?'

He shakes his head. 'There are some who would pour poison into our people's ears.' He tells me that five years before Celine and I were born, people in the village went around terrorising Tutsi families. 'They called them *inyenzi*. Told them to flee or they would be stamped out.' Data said that Celine's parents were forced to move to Burundi in 1973. 'They came back when Celine was five. To take care of her grandmother.'

We sit in the garden for a while longer, dwarfed by the vast expense of cloudless night sky. After a while, I wrap my arms around Data's neck and hug him goodnight.

'Sleep safe,' he says.

The next morning, the boys are already eating when I step into the kitchen. Mama is dancing, as always. She swirls across the room as I sit, perching a kiss on my forehead.

'Good morning, Victoria,' she sings. Her contagious good humour makes me smile. Today is a new day, I think, grabbing a handful of sorghum porridge from the large pot. As I do, the music ends.

'Since when do they have advert breaks on the music channel?' I ask, to no one in particular.

'New radio, sis!' the boys reply, in unison. My hand stops in mid-air. The heavy silence is quickly replaced by a rapid fire of voices debating the Arusha Accords. I search for Mama's eyes, but all I find is her back, still swaying to muted tunes long internalised. The voices on the radio grow louder, denouncing Habyarimana's betrayal of his people. That word again, *inyenzi*. I wish the music would return. The RTLM jingle I heard the day before sounds, echoed by the boys' singing: 'Hutu Power! Hutu Power!', falling over with ugly laughter. My own brothers.

'This is no joke,' I shout, raging at the little transistor, turning its dial to the off position.

'What got into you, my boys?' Mama questions, her body an unfamiliar stillness. Words have infiltrated our homes. Dangerous words. *Interahamwe. Impuzamugambi.* I hear them on the street, at school. In our own kitchen.

'They don't get it, Mama,' I say, turning away from my two brothers before bursting into tears.

It has been a year since that day. Data boxed the boys around the ears and Mama returned to her old radio station. The government has signed the Arusha Peace Agreement to end the civil war and establish a transitional government, with balanced representation

29

from the Tutsi and the Hutu. Since the President signed, Data's office has been handling a series of economic packages to support local businesses. The future of Rwanda, Data calls it.

That morning, the boys have already gone ahead, keen to start their game of football. After breakfast, I meet Celine who is waiting outside. She is dressed in a flowery yellow dress, her hair wrapped in a vibrant purple scarf. It is still the Easter holiday, but today is orientation day in school for our year group. The air is filled with the smell of orange blossom flowers, sweet and joyful. On the way, we walk and talk about our future. I still want to be a translator.

'You only say that because you want to travel,' she teases me. Celine wants to be a historian. Her parents want her to give them grandchildren.

At 9 o'clock, we go in. I look around but find no sign of Benjamin in the playground. The sister has arranged a history talk whilst we wait. At break time, a few boys chase after an old leather ball, Paul amongst them. Near the gate, Celine and I have been asked by the sister to draw the blue, yellow and green flag of Rwanda to welcome the people from the Education Committee coming to assess ten of us for a scholarship. Our teacher said she studied in Paris on one of those scholarships. She said today could be the most important day of our lives. Once we are done with the flag, Celine and I use blue, white and red chalk pieces to draw colourful patterns along the convent wall. They look like ancient warding signs.

After lunch, the sister calls us back into class. 'The Committee is here. In the chapel.' There is a faint murmur in the classroom as the ten pre-selected children stand up to make their way. 'If you wait outside, they will call you one at a time.'

We have been rehearsing for weeks. Ten minutes to say who we are, who we see ourselves becoming and why we would make the best scholarship recipient.

'Make me proud, my children,' she calls after us as we take a step out of the room and towards our future.

Celine and I agree to meet under our tree once the interviews are over. A beige lady with straight blond hair and a clipboard calls out my name. Her formality feels absurd. There are only ten of us. To this blond woman, that's all I am: a name on a list. Ten minutes to decide the rest of my life. My stomach churns. I miss a step. I am going to be sick. From behind me, I hear Celine's voice *'Imana iguhe umugisha* Victoria' – God bless you. I shorten my steps, straighten my back, and raise my head high. When I reach the chapel, I turn towards her. My best friend. Celine has a wide smile on her face as the woman waves me in.

On the other side of the convent wall, the humming of a multitude of little transistor radios has been echoing across the thousand hills that surround us since the night before, swelling into a single voice. 'The private Falcon jet of President Juvénal Habyarimana has been shot down,' the voice announces. On RTLM, the voice turns into an incantation. 'Kill the *inyenzi*! Kill the Tutsi cockroaches!'

I don't know it yet, but in the time it takes for the committee to assess the future of ten children, bands of men in colourful shirts will gather at road junctions. Lazy men drinking beer at first. Angry men with a grudge. Younger men robbed of a future. The radio urges them on. Pangas are handed out as weapons.

I have been waiting under the tree for half an hour when I hear gunshots. I race down to the classroom. Empty. Through the barred windows, I can see men waving machine guns in the air, soldiers. One of them is holding a piece of paper. He appears to be reading names from a list. The sister is standing by the children, a small boy in her arms. Her face is red from pleading with the man in green uniform. He pushes her to one side, she falls. Her white habit is smeared with red earth. The small boy starts to wail. The soldier shouts something to one of the men standing behind him. The man steps forward, raises the handle of his gun and brings it down onto the little boy's skull. The wailing stops, replaced by the sister's scream. I press both hands onto my ears as hard as I can. Forcing my eyelids shut, I hold my breath.

When Data finds me, it is dark. I can no longer see.

'Victoria, I found you. Thank you *Mana*.'

Data pats my body as if to make sure all of me is still here.

'The children?' I whisper, not knowing what I am asking.

'Outside.'

'The boys?'

'They separated the children. All the Tutsi are dead.'

'Celine?' I ask, with a gasp.

'We need to go, Victoria.'

'Data. I need to see.'

'No, sweetheart.'

Data picks me up like a broken doll and carries me away. The smell of his aftershave fills my nostrils. Orange and cinnamon. Risking a look, I don't recognise the road Celine and I took this morning. The air is filled with an acrid smell. Metallic. Hazy.

'Don't look,' Data orders, quickening his pace. I don't understand what I am seeing at first. Everything is out of focus. Then I am able to trace a familiar shape. A leg. But it is all wrong. Then I see them. The bodies.

'Look,' Data whispers. 'We are home now.'

Behind the wood-clad double portal, I picture our garden. This world I thought familiar has been plunged into perpetual night.

32

My eyelids are pressed together so hard that I fear I will never see again.

Data keeps walking, keeps holding me. 'Victoria,' he calls again. 'We're home.'

Slowly, I force my eyelashes apart. The white floodlight of the midday sun burns deep into my retina. I blink and before me Mama appears, dressed in the colour of Rwanda's rich earth, holding on to her crossed elbows. The deep cracks of her face are filled with worry wells, like so many hills. Her smile has gone.

'The boys?' Data asks.

'In the kitchen,' she replies.

'Stay with Victoria,' he tells her, depositing my limp body on the garden bench. As she approaches, I can smell the Macadamia oil she uses to tame her grey curls. Dropping onto the bench with a heavy thud, she places my head on her lap, starts stroking my face. I feel the roughness of this hand so used to grating the cassava. I feel the softness of her love. All I can see are bloodied limbs, dismembered.

Above my head, Mama has started to rock back and forth, attuned to a silent rhythm. I search for another image. A flower. An orchid. I draw the line of each petal from its thin green stem to its speckled yellow pistil, crowned by two kidney-shaped petals the colour of blood. It marks the edge of the path where Celine and I planted it last year for a school project. My eyes fill with tears, blurring the memory.

From the kitchen, an eruption of voices pulls me back. Mama seems deaf to it at first. Only the cadence of her silent grief redoubles.

'What is it, Mama?' I ask.

'Shuuush Victoria, it will all be fine,' she says, as if to someone else. I rise from her lap, pushing aside my tears.

'Of course it will not be fine. Men came to my school and killed children as if they were pests. *Inyenzi*. Cockroaches.' My body starts to shake. 'The road.' I swallow a sob. 'Mama, they were hacked to death.' Mama cups the side of my face with her warm hand, anchoring her eyes into mine, as if to prevent my head from rolling to the ground. I see her tears then.

Behind us, the kitchen door bursts open. My brother Benjamin steps out as if propelled by the Devil. Looking back over his shoulder, he throws words into the kitchen like grenades. As he draws level with us, I feel Mama's hand tensing around my jaw. Taking my eyes off Mama's face, I see it. The panga clasped in his right hand, dripping with blood.

Data appears at the top of the stairs. 'This is not who we are, son,' he pleads. Benjamin looks up. His eyes are bloodshot. I can smell the alcohol on his breath as he replies, 'We have to do our duty.' As he says it, he takes three long strides, pushes the portal open, and disappears into the street.

Mama's hand drops on her lap. '*Imbabazi*,' she whispers. Have compassion.

That night is the 7th of April 1994, four days after Easter. We do not sleep. Instead, Mama, Data and I sit around the kitchen table, my little brother Paul asleep in the room upstairs. We are listening to the broadcast on RTLM urging all Hutu to take arms and do their duty. By morning, the radio broadcasts that the Rwandan Patriotic Army and the Belgian Peacekeepers are responsible for the death of President Habyarimana. Data is on the phone, calling colleagues to find out the truth. When nobody answers, he tells us he has to go out. Mama begs him to look for Benjamin. 'He is only fourteen,' she says. Only a year younger than me. Data promises.

Mama springs into action, getting her cooking pot out, preparing breakfast. I switch off the transistor radio.

'Where is everyone?' Paul asks, rubbing the sleep off his eyes.

'Early start,' I reply, not wanting to alarm him. We sit in silence to eat. Today, there is no dancing. No singing. Even the radio remains mute.

'Who's going to walk me to football if Benjamin has already left?' Paul asks, concerned.

'No football today,' Mama replies, her back to us, her shoulders quivering. I take Paul into the garden to give her a moment and sit him on my lap. He is seven years old. Small for his age. His big eyes still see the world with the blinkers of childhood.

'What happened yesterday?' I ask.

Paul tells me that men came to his classroom. They were looking for Tutsi. 'Benjamin was with them. There was a man I recognised from football. He told Benjamin to take me home.'

'Did he say anything, Paul?' I ask, hoping to understand.

'No, he took me back then went to meet the man from football. He said I wasn't allowed to come,' Paul says, pouting.

I stroke the tight curl on his head. 'It's OK, Paul. I can play with you.' Had Benjamin really returned to the school? I couldn't remember seeing him. All I could remember was the blood dripping from the grass-cutting blade of the panga.

Paul and I play in the garden that morning. In the open-doored kitchen, Mama sits, straight, motionless, watchful. Every so often, a noise drags her watching gaze beyond the wooden portal. She looks into the hills as if cursed with the all-seeing eye. She looks, and then she weeps. In the distance, columns of smoke are striating the cerulean sky, like claw-marks tearing at our land.

Oblivious, Paul dribbles his football around me, moving side to side, swerving to avoid an invisible opponent.

'Come on, Sis. Don't just stand there,' he calls to me.

'You watch!' I reply, picking up my feet. 'Ready or not!'

I start to run, chasing Paul the length of the garden path, calling after him, 'I'm coming!'

'Mama, look. I'm being hunted by a monster,' Paul calls to her, delighted.

Immersed in our game, we fail to see the shift at first. In an instant, Mama is standing, waving at us to come back. Paul readies himself to argue for more time when the portal gate opens onto a man in a green uniform, a shiny leather holster at his belt. Mama is at the bottom of the stairs now, moving towards the man with the stance of a lioness protecting her cubs. I grab Paul, place him against my hip, and walk hurriedly towards the steps. Mama has reached the soldier by the time I turn to look.

'*Muraho, bwana*,' she greets him. '*Amakuru*?'

'*Trés bien, merci*,' he replies in the formal administrative French. '*Et vous*?'

'*Bien, merci*,' she replies, mirroring his choice of language. 'How can I help you today, Colonel?'

'*Ndashaka…*' he hesitates, swaps to French. 'I'm looking for Monsieur.'

'This time of day? Why would you be looking for him at home?' she replies. 'Do you think my husband is a lazy man?'

'Do you know where I can find him?' the man in uniform insists, still speaking French.

'*Simbizi*,' Mama replies. I don't know. '*Wihangane*.' Sorry.

'Tell him, we have been looking. He has work to do. Tell him to find me. We have set up a roadblock near the school.'

'I'll tell him. *Murabeho*,' Mama says. Goodbye.

'*Turongera*,' the soldier replies. I'll see you soon.

I watch, Paul close by my hip, as the man in the green uniform turns on his heels and walks through the gate. Mama seems tethered to the ground for a moment, her shoulders raised high. As I let go of the breath stuck in my lungs, I see Mama's shoulders drop as if they were my own. She covers the few steps to the portal, pushes the gate shut. Only then does she look back. Her face is the face of a ghost.

'Inside, Victoria. You and Paul go inside.'

Without a word, I do as she says. In the kitchen, I place Paul on the bench and hand him a drink of water. The air is strangely still. Outside, Mama has reached the garden bench. She leans on it for a moment, catching her breath, before climbing the few steps to the kitchen door in front of which she sits, guarding us.

Later, once Paul is asleep, I join Mama on the steps. Together we wait as we have done all day, deep into the night. Finally, we hear the creaking noise of the portal being pushed open and shut. Mama searches the shadows for signs of an intruder. Data appears at the bottom of the steps. Mama scans the darkness for signs of Benjamin, but I know he isn't coming back. Not yet. Data drops halfway up the stairs, his back turned to us, resting against Mama's leg. The back of his shirt is heavily crumpled. His trousers are soiled with grass and earth stains at the knee. For a long time, we stay like this. Mama and I at the top of the steps; Data midway. When he finally speaks, his voice seems to come from the darkness below.

'I'm sorry, Victoria,' he says. 'Celine's family. They are all dead.'

I want to scream, but they have stolen the air out of my lungs. For a moment all I can hear is their absence. The birds outside have stopped singing.

'*Wariye?*' Mama asks, breaking the silence.

Data shakes his head: no, he hasn't eaten.

'The *Interahamwe* are everywhere... Bands of drunken men with pangas... They have erected roadblocks... They are checking everyone's ID card... Looking for Tutsi.'

'Benjamin?' Mama asks.

Data shakes his head again. Mama tells of the soldier who came earlier. 'What do they want with you?' she asks, knowing the answer.

'There are no bystanders,' Data replies, 'You are either with them, or another Tutsi cockroach.'

The word in his mouth startles me.

'This is not who we are,' I say, repeating his own words, searching for his eyes.

'All the phone lines have been cut,' Data says, ignoring me. He is looking at Mama intently now. 'At the office too.'

'The soldier will be back,' she replies.

Data stares into the darkness for a very long time. 'Tomorrow, I'll go,' he finally says. '*Ndananiwe*,' he adds, getting up. I am tired. Mama follows him inside, to warm the food she kept for him. I wave at her. I will follow, soon.

Alone, I look up towards the stars, but the night is hooded under the amassing smoke. The smell of corpses baked under the afternoon sun has risen and is filling my nostrils. I don't know why I didn't notice it before. Maybe because I was still waiting, carried by hope. I don't understand what Data is saying, or not saying. I know the hatred has been brewing for decades, encouraged by the Hutu government. It has always been around us. Resentment from the time of the *abazungu*, the White People. Long before I was born. But it was never like that for us. Data taught us differently. We are Hutu, but Mama's mum was Tutsi and so we are a little of both, I guess. Now my best friend is dead, because she was a Tutsi. A name on a list. And Benjamin...

Dropping to my knees, I put my hands together and I call into the dark, like the sisters taught me. '*Imana*. Our Lord, save us all.' But no one is listening.

The scent of sweet cinnamon and bitter orange lingers in the kitchen, although Data has long left for the school compound where the soldier in the green uniform awaits. 'I will reason with him,' he reassured Mama, 'and bring Benjamin home.'

Our kitchen is an island from which we wait for news from Data, for Benjamin's smile, for snippets of information on the radio, drowned amongst the Hutu Power propaganda. When Data returns, the heady vapour of alcohol floating around him makes my eyes water. The radio goes on. In Kigali, Interahamwe and the Presidential Guard work fast, expanding their hunt to the rest of the country, doing their 'duty'. The white people have fled. An interim government has been formed, and soon move from Kigali to Gitarama, pursued by the Rwandan Patriotic Army. The radio talks of a Tutsi invasion from the North, calls on all to defend 'our' land.

That night, Mama asks Data about Benjamin, her raised chin met by tired eyelids, a bowed head, a clenched jaw.

'They know your mother was a Tutsi,' is all he says.

After dinner, Mama wraps Paul into her arms, lifts him into the folds of her boubou, carries him to bed like a baby. Paul is quietly accepting of her strange behaviour. He feels Benjamin's absence too. I watch from the kitchen steps as Data takes his place on the bench outside. Not once does he look up at the stars. He seems in a perpetual haze. I pretend not to have seen the machete he hid under a bush by the garden entrance.

In days to come, I close my eyes when I wash the stains splattered across the front of his shirt. *This is not who we are.* The voice on the radio is pouring lies into our ears. In the confines of our house, all I can do is pray.

Once, when we were in school, one of the boys from football told Celine to go back to her own country. The sister found her crying and told her that before the Belgians came to Rwanda, *Tutsi* was the word for cattle owners. 'We are all one people, Celine,' she told her. 'God's children.'

Celine had dried her tears then and ran to find me. 'This means that we can be sisters, Victoria. See?'

Now Celine is dead, and I feel alone. Hutu Power. Tutsi cockroaches. People killing people for words. I wonder what happened to the sister. Whether she was killed with Celine, or whether the men let her go? I am not so naïve, though. Mama warned me against men who smell of alcohol a long time ago.

'It is as if they are possessed,' she said. 'Stay away from them, always.'

I suddenly think that it would be a relief if they were possessed. If my sweet Benjamin could be saved.

The madness has been raging for ten weeks when Benjamin barges through the kitchen door one morning. I don't recognise him at first. His face is that of an older man, hirsute, rugged and strained, eyes sunken deep into his skull by too many sleepless nights. No longer the face of my little brother.

'Pick up your things! We have to go,' he shouts in my direction.

Mama takes a cautious step towards him. I can see she needs to touch him, make sure he is not a ghost. She moves to hug him, but Benjamin recoils, an air of disgust across his face.

'Not you,' he says.

Mama's face hardens with the blow. Her hand starts to shake. 'Benjamin,' she calls in a mother's stern voice, 'Why are you here?'

Ignoring the question as if it were the dead speaking, he gesticulates towards me, motioning me to hurry. 'Victoria. Go get Paul. We have to go,' he says.

I turn towards Mama who is standing very still in the middle of her kitchen, eyes on her middle child. Without taking my eyes off her, I ask: 'Where have you been, Benjamin? It's been weeks.'

He greets my question with a heavy sigh. Only now do I notice that he seems out of breath.

'What's going on?' I ask. I want him to give me a reason.

'The Rwandan Patriotic Army,' he replies in a staccato voice. 'They are killing *us* now. Go get Paul. You have to come with me, now.'

This means that the rebel army is marching from Burundi to stop the hordes of Interahamwe who are murdering anyone who is a Tutsi. 'What about Mama?' I ask.

Benjamin's jaw clamps in exasperation, the edge of it throbbing. A growling sound escapes from deep inside him, a hunted animal's warning. 'Tell her, woman,' he shouts, staring at Mama now.

The panic in her son's voice seems to hit Mama like lightning. 'Do as your brother says, Victoria.'

I am about to object when Paul appears at the kitchen door, looking for something. He spots his older brother. 'BenBen. I knew you'd come back.' He runs to Benjamin and throws his arms around his neck. For a second, the strain on my middle brother's face seems to ease, so that he looks like himself again. Reassured, I leave them to pack a bag.

'All good?' Benjamin asks as I re-enter the kitchen, Paul sitting astride his shoulders, chattering for the first time since his hero left.

I nod.

'Let's go, kids,' he calls for Paul's benefit, turning towards the door.

'What about Mama?' Paul asks, hanging his face upside down into his brother's face. Benjamin's fist closes. For a moment he looks as if he is going to strike Paul. From behind him, Mama reaches for his hand.

'You go with your brother,' she tells Paul. 'I'll wait for Data.'

Benjamin shakes off her grip, and continues towards the door, without ever looking back. Following behind, I hesitate at the door, but Mama smiles, encouraging. 'It's alright, Victoria. Be a good girl. *Ndagukunda.*'

'I love you too, Mama.'

For days we travel west, Paul, Benjamin and I. We are surrounded by men with bloodshot eyes and machetes, concealed in armoured trucks dressed in the blue, white and red of the French army. On the soldiers' radio, we hear that the interim government has relocated to Gisenyi, chased by the Rwandan Patriotic Army's advance. There are rumours of massacres. The soldiers are talking of tribal war, calling us 'victims'.

Paul keeps asking about Mama and Data. I tell him that we will find out more as soon as we arrive. It feels like we might be running for the rest of our lives. Every few kilometres is a checkpoint, guarded by muddied men with alcohol on their breaths and fear in their eyes. When they see the tricolour flag, they seem to straighten up. 'Vive la France!' they call, waving us on with machine guns and panga blades. In between, are the remnants of *le travail,* as Benjamin called it. Scattered limbs piled on the side of the road. Bloodied clothes, a pregnant woman with her swollen belly hacked off. I shield Paul's eyes with my hand, repressing a wave of sick in my mouth. Benjamin catches my gesture, yanks my hand away.

'Let him look,' he says, a flame dancing in his eyes. 'Let him know what we do to the *Inyenzi.*'

'What happened to you, Benjamin?' I ask one night, immediately wishing I hadn't.

Benjamin stares at me with hatred in his eyes. 'It needed to be done. Don't you see? The *Inyenzi* have been stealing our jobs, our land, treating us like dirt.'

'That's not true, Benjamin,' I reply, imploring. *This is not who we are.*

'You're confused, Victoria,' Benjamin tells me, with the forgiving air of a preacher. 'You'll see, it was all for the best.'

'And Mama?'

He waves his hand in the air to silence me, looking around to make sure nobody heard. 'If you know what's good for you, you'll stop asking questions,' he says, before grabbing a bottle of local alcohol off the floor and walking away. My brother is possessed.

On the third day, we reach the edge of lake Kivu, and the border with neighbouring Zaïre. At nightfall, Benjamin wakes Paul who is asleep on my lap. 'We're here,' he tells him with a smile. 'Get your stuff,' he orders me, before jumping out of the truck.

It is the 14th of July when we arrive. I know because the French soldiers are celebrating Bastille Day. The camp stands beside the town of Goma. For three days, six thousand refugees every hour pour in to the French Safe Zone. The flight of the guilty, I think. For those around me *are* guilty. On crossing the border, we become something else, cleansed by the waters of Lake Kivu. Refugees. But this camp is a sort of purgatory. Here, there is no water, no food, no sanitation.

'We can't stay here,' I tell Benjamin.

'We can't go back out there,' he replies with a groan, pointing at the other side of the lake.

'Are we going to find Mama and Data now?' Paul interrupts.

I crouch down, take his face into my hands. 'Tomorrow, sweet. We'll find someone to ask tomorrow.' When I look up, Benjamin has started to walk towards a line of soldiers sitting behind trestle tables, ignoring the queue. A soldier in the green of the Rwandan Government troops circles around one of the tables, moving towards us. Instinctively, I clasp Paul's hand tighter.

'Benjamin, *mon grand*,' the man calls, wrapping my brother in his bloodied arms as if he was family. 'I'm glad you made it.'

'Colonel, good to see you,' Benjamin replies with a confidence ill-suited to the situation. 'Where do you want us to go?' Benjamin throws his thumb over his shoulder, pointing towards Paul and me.

'*Mais bien sûr*,' the soldier in the green uniform responds.

I realise that this is the man who visited our house in April, looking for Data. With this recognition comes a wave of courage. I step forward, standing alongside Benjamin, Paul still in my grip.

'Excuse me, Sir,' I address the soldier in French. 'We were separated from our parents in transport. Would you know if they have already arrived?'

On hearing this, the soldier shoots a raised eyebrow in Benjamin's direction. Benjamin grabs my arm, recoiling. 'The Colonel is a busy man, Victoria. We don't want to bother him with such details.'

The Colonel nods a sign of approval at Benjamin, gives him the name of someone to find in the camp and gestures him on his way.

'Thank you, Colonel,' Benjamin replies, dragging Paul and me in the direction the man is pointing. Once we are no longer within earshot, Benjamin turns towards me. 'Never mention our parents again,' he whispers in my ear. 'I can protect you, but only if you are not a foolish girl.'

'Let go of me,' I reply, pulling away from his grip. 'You're hurting me.'

The first few days in the camp are a blur. Thanks to the Colonel, we are allocated a tent, supplemented with a small space for cooking. Everywhere around us, people are starving and dehydrated, disease is spreading. Soon, dead children pile up on the side of the road. Nobody to collect the bodies or put them in the ground. It is as if we have left our humanity at the gate. Soon, the Hutu leaders get organised, replicating the Interahamwe factions from back home. Benjamin is one of them. One of the organisers. One of the Colonel's men. People seem to know him. To cower in front of him. To give him the little they have in exchange for protection. I tell myself I am taking the food that belongs to others to feed Paul. As the days go on, I recognise myself less and less.

Then the humanitarian aid starts to come in. Trucks of rice, at first, then logisticians assessing how many toilets, how many graves. Eventually, religious orders send missionaries to provide the adults with solace, and the children with schooling. One morning, as I am preparing breakfast for Paul on the little fire outside our tent, I hear a voice.

'Victoria?'

It has been so long since anyone has called my name that I don't react at first.

'Victoria? Is that you?'

This time I raise my head. I blink to make sure my eyes are not playing tricks on me. The woman in front of me is dressed in a white cotton blouse and long pleated white skirt, smiling, like an apparition.

'Sister?'

'Oh, Victoria, I knew it was you,' she replies, holding my hands in hers, pulling me towards her, hugging me. 'Victoria. And your family?' She asks cautiously, like someone who understands this is not a simple question anymore.

I press my body into her arms, try to speak, burst into tears.

'Oh, sweetheart. It's OK to cry,' she tells me, stroking my hair like Mama used to do.

I cry for a long time, safely in her arms. She lets me.

Later, she tells me that she and the other Sisters were forced to leave, driven in army trucks to Kigali airport by armed soldiers. She speaks of Celine in a soft voice, tells me she is with Jesus now. I tell her about Paul, about Mama and Data left behind. I tell her about Benjamin. At that last part, she frowns.

'We have established a centre for children,' she finally says. 'We have food, and the soldiers leave us be. Would you come? Bring Paul?'

I hesitate. I think about Benjamin and how he will react.

'I could do with your help to teach the younger ones, Victoria.'

I promise to come.

The next morning, as soon as Benjamin has left for his daily round, I dress Paul in a clean shirt, and we walk to the centre together, as if it was a normal school day. On the way, I tell him it is our secret. Make him promise not to mention it to Benjamin. He seems to understand. Paul hasn't spoken since we arrived in the camp. At night, he cries himself to sleep, calling Mama only in his dreams. Sometimes, Benjamin beats him into silence.

When we reach the centre, the sister is there to greet us. She picks Paul up and holds him in her arms, rocking him.

'This is us,' she tells me.

The centre is a large tarpaulin held together with heavy duty ropes that extend to a nearby tree, providing the children with shade from the midday sun. Despite the absence of concrete walls, the place feels insulated from the madness around us. Here, small children sit in a circle, singing nursery rhymes; older children in clean t-shirts sit at individual desks made from wooden boxes painted blue and yellow. After a while, the sister puts Paul down and hands him to a young sister with an angelic face who walks him to a group of children his own age. They are playing a game. I watch as Paul sits amongst them, allowed to be a child for the first time in so long.

'Come with me,' the sister tells me.

I follow her towards a further tent where boys and girls of about ten are receiving a lesson, lined up on a small wooden bench. As we approach, the teacher stops.

'Good morning, class,' the sister says.

A chorus of voices echoes her greeting.

'This is Victoria. She is going to help you practise your languages.' She turns towards me. 'Is that OK with you, Victoria?'

I smile at the class. 'Good morning, children. Tell me all your names.'

The sister and the other teacher leave me with the smiley faces, looking satisfied.

For weeks I teach French and English to a group of twelve children whilst Paul plays with his new friends. At midday, the sisters feed us all. We play together in the afternoon.

'Paul is coming out of his shell,' the sister tells me one day after lunch as we watch him dribbling a football around another little boy.

'I hope so. He's waiting for Mama and Data to find us. I don't know what to say to him.'

'Did you register their names on the board of missing persons?'

'I did, but something in the way Benjamin is behaving tells me we'll never see them again.'

'I understand,' she says with a gentle expression.

That same day, as Paul and I set up to leave, she catches up with us.

'Would you do me a favour, Victoria?'

'Of course.' How could I not?

'I would like you to write a letter in French for me. I'll explain in the morning.'

When we get back to our tent that evening, Benjamin is already there. The stench of alcohol inside the tent is sickening.

'Where have you been?' he asks, looking at Paul.

I squeeze my little brother's hand, pulling him gently behind me. 'Sorry, we just lost track of time.'

'You shouldn't wander, Victoria. It isn't safe here.'

I know he is right about that.

'I might not always be there to protect you.'

I want to know what he means by that. Instead, I say, 'I'll put Paul to bed.'

'Have you ever had a correspondent, Victoria?' the sister asks when I find her the following day. 'You know, a pen pal?'

'I don't think so, no.'

'Would you like one?' she asks with a grin.

'What do you mean?'

'You know, a friend who lives somewhere else, who you can write to about your day... and they write back, telling you about theirs.'

For a moment, I worry she is suffering from a fever. The idea of getting post in this hellhole is ludicrous, no matter what deals the sisters have managed to strike with the *Interahamwe* so they leave us be.

'I think it would be good to practise your written French,' the sister insists, handing me a sheet of paper torn from an exercise book, and a blue crayon.

Incredulous, I take it nonetheless, since she handed it to me. 'What do I write?' I ask.

'Start with who you are. That's always a good start, I find.'

And so, I write, simply:

> *My name is Victoria Umawahoro. I am from Rwanda but at the moment I am staying with the sisters in Zaïre. The sisters are very nice to us. They teach us. They said we could write, so I can practice my French. I want to become a translator, you see. I speak Kinyarwanda, French, and English.*

When I am done, I hand the piece of paper and the crayon to the sister, who folds the sheet and places it inside an envelope, using the crayon to write something on the front.

'Leave the rest to me,' she says. 'Now go and teach your class.'

I am unsure what just happened, but it feels good to imagine my piece of paper somehow floating out of the centre, out of the camp, out of Zaïre, free to travel out of this nightmare.

Outside, I find Paul playing football with the same two boys. He dribbles around them, running skilfully side-to-side.

'Goal!!!!' he yells, beaming.

Delighted to hear my little brother's voice, I clap with the frantic enthusiasm of an Africa Cup fan, waving my fist in a victory circle.

'What are you two doing here?' Benjamin's voice shouts behind me.

Paul stands on the spot, transfixed. In two steps, Benjamin is by me. 'What the hell do you think you are doing? Are you trying to embarrass me?'

'No, no. We… This is just a centre, for the children.'

At this moment, the sister comes out from under the tent. 'Hello Benjamin,' she calls calmly. 'How are you?'

'You?' he replies, waving an angry finger at the sister. 'I thought we got rid of you,' he says, with a rage that makes me wince. 'Stay away from my family,' he spits. 'You two. With me, now!'

Not a word is exchanged on the way back to the tent. 'Stay here,' Benjamin orders Paul, pointing at the place where he sleeps.

I follow him back outside. 'What happened to you, Benjamin?' I rage. 'My dear brother. What have they done to you?'

Grabbing my neck, he pulls me close. 'You don't get it,' he hisses between clenched teeth. 'You're supposed to be the clever girl, but you're nothing more than a Tutsi-lover.'

The stench of his breath makes me want to vomit. I force myself to look into his eyes, looking for a sign of my brother Benjamin, but all I see is death.

'What did you do?' I plead, half in prayer. 'What did you do to Celine?' The question has been stuck in my throat for weeks. Some part of me knows that once Benjamin answers, we will stop being a family.

'I…' he starts. 'They had to die.'

It sounds so final, so simple. That is the inevitability of the Hutu Power message. In Benjamin's eyes, Celine stopped being the girl who held his hand on the way to school when he was little. She stopped being my best friend. She became one of *them*. I look into those eyes, searching for a sign of remorse. All I find is certainty. A certainty older than the both of us.

'Benjamin,' I start, trying to find the right words.

On hearing his name, he throws me to the ground, lands a kick. I curl into a ball, wondering if this violence makes him feel better. *You're supposed to be the clever girl,* he said. I never realised his resentment before. That day at the school… I had been selected. He hadn't. I didn't think he cared. The sound of a skull being crushed echoes in my mind. I press my hands against my ears to make the sound go away. But the sound is in me, forever. Satisfied with my reaction, this man who is no longer my brother leans towards my diminished shape. 'If you are a clever girl, you will do as I say,' he threatens. 'The Colonel is a powerful man. He is part of the *Akazu*.'

On hearing the name, I open my eyes again. They who own Rwanda's wealth. They who drew the French soldiers here. Madame Agathe, the President's wife, and her 'house' of notorious thugs.

'Now you see,' he tells me. 'No more sisters.'

Now I see. Benjamin is not possessed. He made a choice. He is an *icyitso*. An accomplice in the extermination of all Tutsi. After he leaves that morning, I dress Paul and we return to the centre. The sisters have created the only good thing here. A place where Paul can be a child again. He is all that matters now.

'Good morning, Victoria,' the sister says with a welcoming smile. 'Everything all right today?'

I know what she is asking. She saw Benjamin yesterday. She knows what he did. What he is capable of.

'All good, Sister,' I lie, for Paul's sake.

The sister frowns. I have not fooled her. 'They are waiting for you to start a game,' she tells Paul, pointing towards the sheltered area between the two tents.

We watch as he runs towards his friends, then the sister turns towards me. 'Tell me,' she says, indicating a bench under the shaded tree. We sit next to each other, looking towards the little ones. She places her elbows on her knees, resting her chin on top of her hands. 'I'm listening.'

After I finish talking, she rubs her chin on the top of her hands, joined as if in prayer. For a long time, she remains like this, silent. When she finally straightens her back, she lets out a deep sigh. 'It isn't safe for you two here, Victoria,' she says.

'No Sister, you can't send me away,' I implore. 'This… this is all we have.'

She grasps my hand in hers and smiles. 'There is more to life than this camp, Victoria. Have you forgotten already?'

'No… Yes. I guess maybe I have.'

'Let me see what I can do. It will take a little time, but I'll think of something.'

She squeezes my hand before letting go. I don't know how I feel. Her words sound too much like hope and I feel out of practice.

'I'd better go and teach my class,' I tell her, standing up.

'Victoria!' the sister's voice resounds across the courtyard a few days later. She is waving an envelope in her left hand, smiling, triumphant. 'This has come for you, Victoria. From Paris.'

I run towards her, tripping because the sandals on my feet are too big. By the time I reach her, a swarm of curious pupils has gathered around her, wanting to know about *the letter*. Reaching over their heads, the sister hands it to me. I think to put it in my pocket for later, but their inquisitive looks tell of a hunger to know, now. Holding the envelope ceremoniously, I present the perfect turquoise lettering to the crowd. *To Victoria.* The idea of a letter addressed to me by name from beyond this world seems miraculous. The children are pressing against me now, hoping to be the first to catch a glimpse of the contents.

I remember the familiar statistic Data used to encourage our schooling:

'Only thirty percent of our people are literate, Victoria. To read is to make your own destiny. Too many rely on the word of others for the truth.'

What would the Data who uttered those words have made of the man he was forced to become? *This isn't who we are.* Except, in the end, it is.

'Come on children, give Victoria some space.' The sister interrupts my thoughts. Coming out of my daze, I see that she is signalling for everyone to sit down. Obedient, they drop to the floor as one. I am left standing, letter in hand, already at a distance.

'Open it,' the sister encourages, bringing me back.

I place my finger under the glued tongue of the envelope and tear through its length, revealing a pristine sheet of paper, folded in half.

My name is Iris. I was born Paris. Do you have brothers and sisters?

I am an only child. It is quite lonely at times. The sister here said you are in a refugee camp in Zaïre. I can't imagine what it is like.

Only three lines written in French, a thread from a world where I've been told we are usually invisible.

'Time for class, everyone. Off you go!' the sister says, dispersing the crowd. She turns. 'Are you OK, Victoria?'

'What should I tell her? What should I tell... Iris?'

'Whatever you want, Victoria.' As if she is reading my mind, she adds, 'She sees you. She can bear witness.' As she says it, she hands me another sheet of torn paper and the same blue crayon. 'You can use my desk, if you want.'

Dear Iris,
I have two brothers. They are in the camp with me. We were separated from our parents on the way here. The sisters are helping us to locate them.

Dear Victoria,
It must be terrible not to know what happened to your parents. Tell me your brothers' names. Are you close? The sister here said we are both sixteen years old. Are you able to study? Do you need anything?

54

Dear Iris,
My brother Paul is seven, he is small for
his age, and passionate about football.
He has made many new friends here in
the camp. The sisters have set up a place
for us, so we can keep learning. I help out
with the teaching. I was going to become a
translator, but I realise now that Rwanda
needs teachers more than foreign words.

The letters keep coming. Every day, Paul and I walk to the centre. I teach. He plays. Every day, we make sure to leave at three o'clock, to be back at the tent before Benjamin finishes his rounds. All day, he patrols the camp for the General, taking from those who have nothing. In the evening, he plays kickabout with Paul in front of the tent whilst I prepare dinner from the scraps he brings home. I no longer ask where from. Paul is getting stronger, a little keener to forgive every time Benjamin passes the ball, a little less deaf to the words of hatred he shares with us over those meals. He no longer asks about Mama. All around us, he sees the effect of our forced exodus. The lack of food, the dispersed families, the violence. He no longer closes his eyes to avoid the piles of diseased corpses at the side of the road. He knows that the militiamen leave us be because of Benjamin, and his association with the Colonel.

Still, Paul keeps my secret. The letters stay hidden in a tin box the sister gave to me. It used to contain pictures of her family. Her parents, and her twin sister.

'Where is she now, your sister?' I ask, as she pockets the photograph.

'She is doing her noviciate. Two sisters becoming Sisters. It used to make our mother laugh.' She stops, seeing the hurt on my face.

'No news?' she asks, clutching my hand.

I shake my head. Her eyebrows quiver. 'I almost forgot; you've had another one.' She hands me the letter.

The letters with their news from Paris are like little islands in a sea of madness. Sometimes it is hard to believe Iris is real, not a figment of my imagination. After all, how could we have found each other? Our letters are like those messages in a bottle tossed into the sea, travelling thousands of kilometres at the vagary of some unknown force, yet defiant, destined to be found. The sister says God has a purpose for us all.

'What was his purpose when he let Celine be murdered?' I ask.

She replies with her silence, eyes fixed on the ground. I guess she must be wondering the same thing. I watch as her face tightens. She presses her lips so hard against each other that only a straight white line is left.

'This place is not safe Victoria. You know that, right?' she lets it out without taking a breath.

'I know, and I don't know,' I tell her. 'Benjamin...' my voice runs out of air. What I mean to say is that Benjamin's association with the Colonel seems to keep us safe, but that the longer we stay the more I worry I will lose Paul. Instead, all I say is '... Paul.' She understands. I know she does.

'I've asked around,' she continues, as if she has been rehearsing what to say. 'Your father is alive...in Rwanda.'

I raise an eyebrow.

'Mama?'

No, her strained face tells me. 'The militiamen... They came an hour after you left with Benjamin. I am sorry this happened to you Victoria.'

My body is rocked by a deep spasm. I am convinced Benjamin *knew* they were coming. Still, he left her behind, didn't tell her to hide. In my heart, I knew I would never see Mama again. Now my whole body fills with her absence, a silent rage swelling into my ears.

'Why?' I ask in a whisper. The sister squeezes my shoulder, her eyes reaching for my pain like an animal licking a wound, waiting.

'You told me the Colonel visited your house, looking for your father?' she asks after a while, as if gently birthing an idea.

I frown. I recall Paul and I playing in the garden that day, Mama's reaction, the Colonel's veiled threat when he left. After that, everything changed. Data changed.

I look at my watch. Almost three. We are late. I stand and leave the sister behind, under the shade of the big tree. I call Paul. He joins me on the walk home. Today, I forget to ask Paul about his day. Instead, I march ahead, stumbling a few times over my oversized sandals.

'Victoria?' he calls to me.

Startled, I stop and turn back, looking at this handsome little boy with his large eyes filled with softness.

'Is everything OK?' he asks, scrutinising my face.

I force myself to smile. Reassured, he steps forward, takes hold of my hand. We walk the rest of the way side-by-side. Before we get to the tent, I drop to my knees, facing him so that our eyes are level. He looks frightened. Maybe he knows what is coming next. I try to remain stoic, to make him feel safe.

'Paul, my lovely boy, Mama isn't coming back,' I blurt out, tears rolling down my cheeks. I wrap my arms around him, pull him to my chest, wanting to absorb all his suffering. I am surprised by the stiffness in his body. He must be holding his breath.

'I promise I'll never leave you, Baba,' I whisper.

Behind me, I hear Benjamin calling. When I let go of Paul, I see that his jaws look cast in iron. His wide eyes are locked onto his brother.

'What are you two doing?' Benjamin asks with a scoff.

Ignoring the question, I hurry Paul into the tent. 'Change your clothes before dinner,' I tell him.

Outside, Benjamin waits, eyeing me with suspicion. As I approach, he hands me a ripped plastic bag filled with provisions.

'For dinner,' he says.

In the bag, I find a whole cassava. A rare treat. I get busy with pots and pans, washing, grating, shaping a meal out of disparate ingredients. All the while, he stands behind me.

'Where have you been today?' he asks, twirling the edge of his colourful shirt between his thumb and his finger.

'You know, here and there,' I reply, keeping to my preparations. I feel an iron grip on my lungs.

'The Colonel needs a cook,' Benjamin says. 'I told him you were very good.'

The grip tightens, preventing me from breathing freely. *No,* I think.

'That's very kind, Benjamin,' I force myself to say. 'But I can't. Who's going to take care of Paul if I have to cook for the Colonel?' Before he answers, I know what Benjamin is about to say. The tightness is in my throat now.

'That's OK,' Benjamin replies. 'Paul can come with me…'

'No!' I shout, turning to face him. 'You can't. He's only a child.' My ears resonate with the pounding from my chest. My little brother. 'You…' I start.

'Stop treating Paul like a baby, Victoria,' he roars. 'Look around you. Look where we are. He has to toughen up. We all do.'

'No!' I shout louder, hoping to summon Mama's accents of authority. Softening my voice, I step towards Benjamin and place my hand on his shoulder. With only two years between us, there is not much difference in our heights. Still, I am the eldest. 'You and Paul are my responsibility, Benjamin. We don't have to stay in this hell. I can take care of you both.' As I say the words, my voice steadies. I hope to remind him, to conjure up the old Benjamin. 'We are family.'

'What are you talking about,' he growls, stepping away from my grasp. 'Who have you been plotting with?' He narrows his eyes. 'I knew it was a bad idea to bring you. I told the Colonel you were always an *Inyenzi*-lover.' As he says it, he pushes me backward and I fall. 'They say it runs in families through the women.'

'Nonsense,' I reply. 'You are a quarter Tutsi too.'

Rage distorts the face hanging over me.

'Silence, woman!' he roars, hitting me with the back of his hand. And, more quietly, he says, 'Don't let anyone hear you say that here,' looking furtively for witnesses as he speaks.

From inside the tent, Paul emerges, running. He sees me on the ground. In his hand is Benjamin's panga. Before either of us can do anything, he raises the long blade and brings it down with all his force onto Benjamin's clenched fist, slicing the hand clean off.

My ears resonate with my little brother's guttural scream, overlaid with Benjamin's cry of pain. Too much noise. I look around. People are starting to gather. I raise myself from the ground, rush towards Paul, grab the blade from his shaking fingers. 'Quick, Paul. We can't stay here,' I say, grabbing his hand and dragging him after me.

We race between the tents, jumping over cooking pots and buckets full of dirty laundry, chased by a mounting clamour of people as they reach the back of our tent to find Benjamin, prostrated, his hand missing. My head thumps with the urgency. I need to take my little brother to safety. There is only one place. On a normal day, the walk takes twenty minutes along the main road. Still running, we cut through the area behind the latrine where the sister warned girls off drunken men looking for love; across the mass grave where diseased bodies wait to be covered in lime in deep communal holes, fetid with the rotting smell of fermented beans. Finally, we reach the compound of the centre. Crossing the playground, we ignore the startled children calling our names, rushing to the smaller tent at the back of the teaching space.

'Please, help us,' I beg, tumbling into the sister's tent. 'I can't lose him too.'

I drop to my knees at the feet of the sister, still grasping Paul's hand. Paul, whose body has taken on a floppy consistency. For a moment he hovers over me, before losing consciousness and dropping into my arms. Lifting his listless body towards the sister, I look up at her comforting white shape, blurred by my tears. 'Please save us.'

After I barge into her tent, the sister scoops Paul out of my arms and lifts him over her shoulder, patting his back as she orders me to follow. We walk along a gravelled lane leading from the back of the centre, towards the tree line that marks the edge of the camp, and into the thick woods beyond. My steps echo the gentle tapping of her hand onto Paul's inert body, soothing my fitful heartbeat. Ahead of us, the sun has started to set when we reach a village hanging over lake Kivu. It occurs to me we might no longer be in Zaïre. The sister directs us towards a small hut with a corrugated roof in the style of many Rwandan homes.

She taps at the door, stained with powdered ochre. Inside, some-one shuffles towards the entrance like a wounded animal. I must look weary, for the sister smoothes the hair off my face.

'It's going to be OK,' she says.

The door opens onto a dark space. The sister encourages me in, stepping after me. I blink so my eyes can get accustomed to the darkness. Behind me, a shadow pushes the door shut before pointing at a single bed on the other side of the hut.

'You can put him there,' the shape says to the sister in a voice that makes me shiver.

'Data?' I ask in disbelief. 'Is that really you?'

We sit around a small wooden crate that serves as a table. The sister tells us we have much to discuss and leaves, promising to return later. I watch Paul as he sleeps peacefully for the first time in months, and wonder if, somehow, he can feel Data's familiar presence.

'How?' I ask once I am able to stop staring. Data's face is emaciated, his eyes sunken and his lips cracked. His left thigh is wrapped in a dirty cloth stained with blood, secured with what I recognise to be his old leather belt. Questions collide in my mind. *Your father is still in Rwanda*, the sister said. Had he been less than two hours away all this time?

'Why did you not come to find us in the camp?' I ask. 'We thought you were dead.' A sob rolls out of my throat then, robbing me of words.

Data pulls me towards him, wrapping me in his wiry arms. We stay like this, with him holding me, me curled up into his chest, balancing on his good leg, my face buried in his shirt. He smells sour, no longer of orange and cinnamon, but like death, as if when I move, his ghost will vanish.

The sound of the closing door startles me. I feel Data's grip loosen around me as he looks up.

'Have you not moved since I left?' The voice of the sister rings soft with understanding.

I feel Data shake his head.

'Come on, sweetheart,' the sister tells me, laying her hand on my shoulder. 'I need to take a look at that leg.' She gently directs me to a wooden stool next to the crate, then hands me the tin box with my letters. 'Keep these,' she says before kneeling in front of my father, placing the small bag she has been carrying next to her on the floor.

'Let's see,' she says, removing the tourniquet and unwrapping the damaged leg.

Data winces. The sister reveals a deep gouge running across Data's blackened thigh. Pus oozes from the wound when she presses the edges. The smell makes my eyes water.

'So?' Data asks the sister.

'Not good,' she replies. 'The wound has turned to gangrene.'

I watch as the sister cleans the wound as best she can, wrapping a clean dressing over the necrotic tissues. When she is done, Data looks towards Paul, who is still sleeping. 'We don't have much time, Victoria. You must have many questions, but here is what you need to know.'

Data tells me that when the President's plane was shot down, he was in his office. Realising what was about to happen, he took some documents out of the Prefecture where he worked. They showed that the Government had been planning a genocide for decades, compiling lists of Tutsi and undesirable Hutu. The documents showed clear intent, rather than the spontaneous ethnic war the international press had been broadcasting for months.

'The orders from Kigali bore the Colonel's signature,' he continues. 'I thought with these documents I could protect my family.'

'But then the Colonel came to our house,' I interrupt.

'He did. He already knew about your mother, and when I went to the School, he gave me an ultimatum. Benjamin had already joined his militia. The risk was too great.' His voice wavers. I try not to think about what he is implying. The sister places her hand on his shoulder.

'God will judge you for what you did,' she says. 'For now, we must hurry.'

She explains that when the Colonel realised the Rwandan Patriotic Army was pushing them to the frontier, he used his contacts in the French administration to secure the militia's retreat.

'Under cover of the humanitarian zone, they helped those who perpetrated the genocide against the Tutsi escape,' she says.

'The Colonel is a cautious man. He sent Benjamin to collect you and your brother so that I wouldn't send the documents to the UN,' Data explains. 'I will burn in hell for what I did, but he will face the justice of men,' he says, looking the sister in the eyes.

He knew the Colonel would end up in Goma and would order Benjamin to bring Paul and I to him, as a guarantee. Data travelled within reach of the camp, chased by the Colonel's militiamen. I wonder for a moment if Benjamin was one of them.

'That's when I got wounded,' he says. 'Not before I was able to transmit a message to the Centre. I knew she would find you,' he says, smiling at the sister.

'And now, we need to take you both to safety,' she says. 'The Colonel's men are searching the camp for you. It won't be long before they search the centre.'

'My God, we've put everyone in danger,' I exclaim.

She pats my shoulder. 'It's OK,' she says. 'There's a truck that can take you and Paul to the border with Uganda. Someone will be waiting there. We have to leave now.'

'Paul and I?'

Data and the sister exchange a glance. 'I have some unfinished business here, Victoria. I'll join you two later.'

I look at his bandaged leg and I see what is to come. 'At least let me wake up Paul,' I say.

A few hours later, the sister takes me and Paul to a Mercedes truck with huge wheels. Two men are unloading bags of rice and medical equipment into another vehicle.

'My children,' she says, pulling us into her clean embrace. 'I'll miss you so much.'

She lifts Paul onto the back of the truck and turns towards me. 'For what he has to do, your father needs to know you are safe,' she tells me.

'I understand,' I reply. 'Please take care of him, Sister.'

'When you get to Uganda, someone will be waiting for you. Someone close,' she says, handing me a piece of paper.

Turning it over, I realise it is an old picture. I have seen it before. 'Your sister?'

'She'll be there,' the sister confirms with a movement of her chin. She kisses the top of my head. 'Off you go, now,' she says, as if I will be seeing her in the morning.

I have lost so many already. I throw my arms around her white habit and squeeze her body with all my strength. 'I love you,' I tell her.

'I love you too, child,' she replies. 'Now go.'

I climb into the back of the truck and the engine comes to life, shaking our bones.

We ride five hundred and seventy kilometres in two days, stopping only for the two men in the front cabin to alternate behind the wheel. All I know is they are white and one of them carries a gun. They drive us along the border between Rwanda and Zaïre, avoiding checkpoints, as if the devil was on our tail. Most of the time, Paul is asleep on the hot metal bed. When he emerges, he gathers his limbs into a ball and stares at the cloud of dust which rises in our wake like hungry ghosts. He hasn't said a word since we left the camp. He wouldn't let Data hug him, as if convinced the desiccated man was a spirit intent on tormenting him. After a few weeks in the haven of the centre, Paul was much better, I have to remind myself.

When the rattling stops, I notice we are driving on a tarmacked road. The scale of the place is like nowhere I've ever been. I look wide-eyed at the modern buildings, the young men playing football, the girls walking in groups, laughing. A green sign with the logo of a giraffe proclaims *Kampala International University*. In the distance, I see a huge body of water: a road sign tells me it is Lake Victoria. The truck has joined a big artery now, moving away from the capital, towards another sign. Entebbe International Airport. The truck drives to a hangar adjacent to the main airstrip. A white and blue UN flag drapes its front, whilst little ant-like lines of people load other trucks, identical to the one we are riding on. We come to an abrupt halt and I hear the door of the front cabin open and close. The head of one of the drivers emerges from the left.

'That's you,' he says in English.

'Thank you,' I reply in my best English. And turning towards Paul, 'Time to go, little man.'

The sunbathed tarmac feels hot under my feet. It emits a smell of burnt plastic. I look left and right, not sure where we are supposed to go. The driver has disappeared already, no doubt making arrangements for his truck to be re-loaded. Now what? In my pocket, I can feel the photograph the sister gave me. I pull it out, as if it could give me a clue about what we are expected to do now. The image of Data in the hut lingers in my mind. His presence felt like a miracle, but here in Uganda where we don't know anyone it only serves to reinforce how alone we have become. I grip Paul's hand. Then I see her, the lady from the picture. Dark wavy hair, jeans and a baggy knitted jumper at odds with the sweltering heat rising from the ground. She is standing ten paces away, smiling at us.

'Victoria?' She moves closer. 'You kids made it, oh I'm so glad.' She grabs us both and presses us against her chest as if we were long lost relatives. 'I'm so glad,' she says again in French.

Afterwards, she takes us inside the airport hangar, hands us a bag with some fresh clothes and directs us towards a small bathroom at the back.

'It isn't much, but I'm sure you'll appreciate a shower,' she smiles, apologetic.

I can't remember the last time I had a shower. Paul and I go in. Two children emerge an hour later, clean but frightened. Paul is wearing a bright green t-shirt and yellow Bermuda shorts, and I am in a pale blue summer dress. The only thing that gives us away is the state of our feet.

'We'll have to fix that when we arrive,' she says, pointing at the broken buckle of my sandal, and Paul's bare feet.

'When we arrive where?' I ask, still not sure what to expect.

'Europe, Victoria. I was told to take you as far away as possible. It is all arranged.' She hands me another bag. This one contains sandwiches and two bottles of lemonade. 'For the plane,' she says.

We are loaded on a chartered plane. As we take off, I look through the oval window at the red earth moving away from us. The colour of home. The colour of blood. I know in that moment I will never again set foot in Rwanda.

Iris

The humming of the washing machine pulsated in cadence with the thumping in my chest. Through the round window, I watched the reusable nappies complete their cyclical revolutions, compacted against the edge of the drum. The green glow of the digital timer came in and out of focus, slowly morphing into a hazy cloud. My eyelids drooped with sleep.

I found myself in the dark. All around, muffled sounds failed to reach through the deep velvet of artificial silence. A bottle-green light revealed rows and rows of empty burgundy seats, spectator seats. I blinked, willing my eyes to find the timer. Instead, I caught a familiar scent. *Andropogon muricatus*. Vetiver. An essential oil with healing properties. I read somewhere that it promotes the growth of new tissues by replacing the dead ones, keeping a wound safe from infection. Terre d'Hermès. My dad's scent. I leant towards the fragrance, feeling for the pressure of his lips against my forehead. The window of his pager lit up green. I heard the sigh, the zip as he closed his jacket, the creaking of the fold-up seat. I knew he was gone.

I rubbed my eyes raw. Ophelia was standing in the door frame, hugging her stuffed rabbit. She moved towards my spot on the cold kitchen floor, climbed into my arms, curled up into a warm ball, wedged into the fold of my elbow.

'Did you have a nightmare, baby?'

She threw both arms around my neck in silent desperation. Adopting the universal language of motherhood, I cupped her head in the safety of my hand, soothing her fine hair. My body started rocking, as the familiar intensity of maternal love swelled in my chest. Unconditional love. The memory of my own father grazed me. I adored him. I tried to reconcile this conviction with the implication of that single green glowing light. My father was a quiet man. Now that he was gone, all I had was the certainty of my own disquiet.

Something happened in those days of death, when my father worked for the Ministry. The overseer of a dysfunctional relationship between France and Francophone Africa, born out of a strange Franco-French inferiority complex, symptomatic of a rising Anglo-American influence which underlined the end of France's colonial hegemony. One minute he was there... I remembered vague explanations of *genocides*, plural, as we watched news of mass graves unfolding on the evening bulletin. I didn't know then what I did now, about the semantics of genocide. I didn't know about the misguided deterministic colonial meddling, or about its appropriation by a minority, thirsty for power. All I knew was a name: Victoria.

Dear Victoria,
My Dad works for the French government.
They have set up a crisis unit and they are
planning how best to help your people.
Maybe he knows someone who can help you
find your parents? Would you like me to ask?

Dear Iris,
It already seems incredible to have found
each other. Don't worry about us. There are
many French soldiers here, and humanitarian
people from all around the world. Paul and

I have food, and we are lucky that the sisters care for us. Tell me about Paris? Do you live close to the Eiffel Tower?

Dear Victoria,
Paris is big, white and sunny. The official buildings are coated in gold leaves and when the sun shines, it makes everything look majestic. I don't know if I told you, but we have a dog and so I spend a lot of time walking in the Trocadero Park, by our apartment. It overlooks the Eiffel Tower, so I see it every day. Did you know that it is really a lightning rod? What about your other brother? You didn't tell me his name.

Dear Iris,
I didn't know about the Tower. That's funny. Do people really come from thousands of miles to look at a lightning rod? We have those in Rwanda too! As for my brother, his name is Benjamin. He is my middle brother and we used to be very close, but something happened to him. I don't recognise him. He works for this scary man, the Colonel. There is a sister who takes care of us though. She is the one who brings me your letters.

Dear Victoria,
It can't be easy for her to get stamps in the camp. What is your sister like? The ones in

*my school are old women with hairy legs
and grey jumpers. Their nunnery is adjacent
to the school and I sometimes think they live
in a bubble untouched by the real world.
Everyone says some of the nuns haven't been
out for decades. Rumour has it that if they
step over the threshold they will turn into
dust.*

*Dear Iris,
You make me laugh. It feels so good to
laugh. They sound more like witches, your
Sisters. Ours come from all four corners
of the world, and I am amazed that they
somehow ended up here, with us. I think
maybe they are guardian angels sent by God
to protect us.*

*Dear Victoria,
I have a surprise for you. I have been to
the Embassy to get you stamps so we can
continue to write to each other. Three
hundred stamps that I am sending to you
now.*

*Dear Victoria,
Two months without any news. I must
have offended you with the stamps. Please
accept my apologies. I was trying to help.
In my enthusiasm, I didn't stop to think how
it might look. I also forgot to send you a*

picture. Maybe that is what upset you. I am
sending one now. Please write soon.

Dear Victoria,
The sisters wrote to say you have been
moved. They sent back my last two letters. I
am writing again. I wrote on the envelope,
asking them to forward this one to you. As
soon as you are settled, please let me know.
In the meantime, I will continue to write via
the sisters.
PS: Maybe in the move you will find your
parents. I certainly hope so.

Dear Victoria,
The news headlines keep mentioning mass
graves. Please take care of yourself. My
mum says you are welcome to stay with us in
Paris.

I lied to Victoria about those stamps. I didn't know why. I was enjoying her letters. I didn't want them to stop. Maybe I wanted her to think me brave. As brave as a teenage girl in a refugee camp, on the edge of a volcano. The truth was, I asked my father to help. He said he would see what he could do. One night he came home from work with a large brown paper envelope.

'Some stamps,' he said, dropping them on the bed without meeting my eyes. When I opened the envelope, it contained three sheets of Rwandan stamps. Three hundred in total. I had always thought my father to be an important man, a principled man. In the face of political genocide, he turned out to be just a man. Maybe meek, maybe naïve. It was hard to tell. Years later, I realised just how hollow his gesture had been, since the camp of Goma was not in Rwanda but in neighbouring Zaïre.

'That's all I could do,' he told me that night, before closing my bedroom door. In those words, I read the impotence of a bystander. I felt his shame, and it was his shame which was now haunting me.

Mea culpa, mea culpa, mea magna culpa. The sisters taught us that redemption comes with the beating of our chests. For twenty years, I blocked all memory of you, of our letters, of those stamps. Long before Ophelia was born, my father lost his mind. I felt like my heart would explode. The doctors couldn't agree on a diagnosis after twelve days of forced internment. There was much speculation. At one point, my mother floated the idea that his mental breakdown could be work related. 'Some violence he witnessed,' she suggested.

Or maybe a sort of trauma brought on by violence he could not stop, I thought. We both knew of an unspoken truth. In the end, he died. It was like losing him a second time. My mother and I never spoke of it again. I moved to the UK, placing some distance between his death and my life. Running away.

Ten years passed. I was attending a class on automatic writing, training to become a journalist, when Victoria surfaced out of my subconscious. My Rwandan penfriend. The written words brought tears to my eyes as I read them out loud. Another student on the course had worked for an NGO, had been to Rwanda. Some odds. She gave me a phone number. Told me someone could help me find out what had happened. I was too scared to know. I moved to a new house. Lost the number. Life went on. I told myself there was hope in the not knowing. Maybe the sixteen-year-old me *wanted* to believe that only a tragedy could have prevented Victoria from writing. The same moral protectionism with which international institutions justified their inaction, that which drove my father mad. I thought about Candide's 'we must cultivate our garden'. I thought that, indeed, not everything was well in this world.

In the morning, Henry found us both on the kitchen floor, asleep in front of the idle washing machine. He frowned at me. 'What are you two doing there?'

I reached towards the door of the washing machine, pulled it towards me. The soggy nappies fell to the tiled floor like a sad deflated monster. He sighed, picked them off the floor, hung them on the radiator.

'They won't be dry until tomorrow now,' he complained.

'Sorry. I fell asleep.'

'Maybe you should take a break from the writing project,' he replied. 'You know, be present for Ophelia and me a bit more.'

'That's not fair,' I told him without much conviction.

'It is getting to you though, isn't it?' he said, leaning over the kitchen sink where he was peeling carrots and cutting them into strips for Ophelia's packed lunch. 'I mean. All those books about genocide you're reading… It can't be good for you. You've been immersed in it for eight months now. That's all I'm saying.'

I shrugged my shoulders. 'I just need fresh air. That's all.' *I am lying to myself now.* I stretched my back, woke Ophelia, carried her to her highchair. 'You know what *is* hard?' I asked, harnessing her to the chair. 'The names. The names mentioned in the reports about France's responsibility. They're all familiar names. Some of them were people from my dad's work. I feel like I knew them. They probably came to our house for dinner.'

'That can't be easy,' he said. His conciliatory tone was taunting.

'It's like... Well, it's like discovering that your father might have had a hand in the death of over eight hundred thousand people,' I said, a little too loud.

'Right,' he replied, still peeling.

'How can you be so calm?'

'What would you like me to say?'

'That's it!' I reached for my coat and yanked at the sleeve, knocking the breakfast chair off balance. 'Don't wait to eat,' I spat, heading for the door. Behind me, the kitchen chair came crashing down. Ophelia's mounting cry resonated in my ears. Henry put the peeler down, moving towards her.

'Don't!' I told him. 'I've got this.' I tossed my coat on the floor, unshackled a hysterical Ophelia from her watchtower and brought her close to my chest. Her hair smelt of clean soap and sour milk. I lost myself in the safety of that aroma, swaying from the hips. Ophelia's cries receded, her silence masked by my own rising sobs.

My father encouraged the use of a dictionary to gain a greater understanding of the world. He called it *looking for the essence of things*. When I returned from the nursery, the house was empty. Conflicting thoughts crowded my mind. I knew I wouldn't be able to write. I headed for the little office space lodged in one corner of our kitchen, paused in front of the bookshelves, pulled out a copy of the Merriam-Webster dictionary. Flicking to the letter 'G', I searched for the meaning of 'guilt'. The first definition mentioned a breach of conduct violating the law and involving a penalty.

Walking to the desk, I searched in my notebook for a quote I had jotted down the previous week. Eventually, I found it: *The cells in the United Nations detention facility in Arusha house the world's worst criminals. The engineers of a new Holocaust, they planned the genocide with the utmost cunning. They live comfortably though; their compound has gardens, a gym, and they eat fresh food and vegetables.* I stared at the words, written in English. I thought about Victoria, about those children in the camp, most of them forgotten victims. I returned to the definition. Guilt was also the state of one who had committed an offence, *especially consciously.*

My eyes were drawn towards another quote I had circled from Conspiracy to Murder, a book by journalist Linda Melvern. *The Arusha prisoners remain convinced of the rectitude of their actions. They claim the Tutsi are the masters of deceit and accuse them of undertaking a campaign to compare themselves with the Jews in order to get sympathy.* My throat tightened at the obscenity of the accusation. Perpetrators posing as victims. I had read that a few years after the genocide, *Gacaca* courts were introduced to expedite the processing of more than 100,000 cases related to the genocide – too many to pass through the Rwandan justice system. *Gacaca* courts allowed the community itself to hear confessions so the perpetrators could be absolved. The only way to re-unify a country, the government had said. A policy of enforced silence masquerading as a mechanism to bring closure to the community. My Western mind, filled with tales of justice and retribution, failed to comprehend the implications of neighbours living alongside those who murdered their whole families, encouraged to smile, forced to keep quiet. Survivors, resented for being there, still.

The nuns taught me that *guilt* was associated with feelings of regret, remorse, and repentance. The Holy Confession. Amongst the elite who orchestrated the genocide, men were pleading guilty of mass extermination, whilst blaming the victims for their actions.

Harder to comprehend still was the behaviour of the international community. Twenty years on, national and international committees sporadically reviewed the events which led to Rwanda. Men in grey suits and rimmed glasses heard the evidence from those who saw, who ran, who survived. Afterwards, they crafted obscure recommendations, fashioned from empty words, before retreating behind intricately carved doors. Books had been written. Good books. Comprehensive in their allegations. Sincere in their desire to apportion blame. Tolerated because in truth, it was too late. Governments had changed, people moved on.

President François Mitterrand had stepped down a year after Rwanda. Cancer. He died in 1996, never really challenged for the decisions surrounding those hundred days.

The attempts by successive governments to clarify, to understand, to explain, had felt unconvincing, cynical even. It was easy to point the finger at the guy standing behind you in line, but it made it less about understanding a mechanism than about rising above 'those guys.' Those same institutions that were set up after World War Two to prevent a repeat of the Holocaust had failed Rwanda. Something about the perception of a people.

The same colonialist mentality which had driven Mitterrand to condone genocide to protect his dissolving Francophone empire had made it easy for the international press to depict Rwanda as an ethnic war, a backyard brawl not worthy of international intervention. What was at stake was the survival of a failing post-colonial empire, threatened by its Anglophone counterpart. Negligible – so small or unimportant, of so little consequence as to warrant no attention. We had neglected the people of Rwanda.

'I can't find out whether my father had any direct responsibility in what happened in Rwanda, or whether he was swayed by the rhetoric of the time,' I told my magazine editor. 'This is driving me crazy.'

Kerstin had called to check whether I was on schedule to deliver the long-form article I had promised her weeks ago.

'I see,' she replied, her usual inscrutable self. 'How's Ophelia? Is she enjoying nursery?'

'I…' For a moment I couldn't find the words. 'Yes, it's great. I mean, she's loving it.'

'But?'

Kerstin had been my editor at the magazine for a decade now. She knew me better than anyone.

'It's putting a strain on our marriage…' I tried to gather the right words. 'He's English; he doesn't get what's rattling me so much. He *expects* the Frogs to behave badly. It isn't his precious Britain that's on the stand here.'

'You mean he doesn't have your emotional attachment to all this?'

'Yes, and it's making me so angry! He doesn't get it.'

'That it's precisely the same kind of indifference that led to the genocide?'

'Yes,' I said, meekly.

'Iris, sweetheart. You're writing an article about whether his father-in-law was somehow implicated in mass murder. Your husband is a solicitor for whom reputation is key. He might not exactly be jumping for joy, don't you think?'

'I… I guess.'

'We Brits don't really like washing our laundry in public, you know.'

'And I'm enjoying this?'

'Hey, don't shoot the messenger, sweetheart. I'm just saying, have you tried asking him how *he* feels about all this?'

'Not really, to be honest. We've been at each other's throats, and Ophelia…'

'Right, how about I give you an extension? Give you time to talk things through.'

Kerstin was right. I didn't stop to think about how this would impact on him, on us as a family. I had something to prove. To myself, and to everybody else. I needed to show *them* that I could do it all. The marriage, the baby, the career. Ten years I had been writing for the same magazine, commissioning pieces on a range of human-interest pieces, waiting for the right story to propel me above the rest. Then there was the maternity leave, and the sudden feeling that maybe that was it. Without the daily rhythm of the newsroom, I was left with all that doubt. Constantly confronted by my own thoughts. The niggling uncertainty that maybe I couldn't write anything that mattered. That's when I had fished out the folder. Stories from my student days. There she was, amongst some scrap papers. Victoria. Three hundred words written a decade earlier, about an African penfriend I never met, and some letters we exchanged for a while. The fact that the letters had just stopped felt like a metaphor for my own failure to write something *significant*.

This article had been a misguided obsession, I realised. I didn't want to know what happened to you, Victoria. Not really. This wasn't some sort of fairy tale I could read to Ophelia at bedtime. I was not some shining rescuer, and ours was not a happy ending. In fact, there was no ending to this story. Just as there was no real beginning. You were a moment in time. It was not for you that I trawled through thousands of pages of commission reports, articles, witness accounts, eyes jumping from one name to the next, searching for a familiar name to disprove a lingering suspicion. It wasn't your name I was searching for amongst the pages. I was at life's midpoint, a scrivener defined by association. Someone's wife. Someone's daughter. It wasn't guilt that had made me start this project. It was the promise that guilt had to offer. A neatly packaged narrative of trauma, escape; redemption even. By over-inflating my retrospective sense of guilt, I had thought I could create a story with a Hollywood ending.

> *Once upon a time, there was a little girl, somewhere in Africa. Bad men came to hurt her and her family. She ran. They pursued her. Thankfully, she had a guardian angel, who helped her escape. The end.*

Everyone would be happy. The difficult questions would remain unanswered. My editor would get a nice tale for next week's edition. A handful of people might read it. If I did my job well, they might even shed a tear. Then they would step into a consultation room somewhere; nod yes to the head massage; lick the mayonnaise off their fingers before closing the lid of their sandwich box and walk back to their desk.

I rang back to share my reservations with Kerstin.

'Don't be a fool,' she said. 'This is a great story.'

'But…' I tried to object.

'No. Do you *know* how topical this is?' Her voice had taken a higher pitch. 'Someone needs to raise awareness of what happened, to break the silence. Who better than you to do that?'

So why did it feel so wrong, I wondered, ending the call without saying goodbye. Behind me, I heard a shuffling sound. I turned to look. Ophelia was standing behind me, framed in the light from the corridor.

'Are you OK, sweet pea?' I asked, seeing her chewing on her pink blanket. 'Do your teeth hurt?'

Ophelia waddled towards me, slobbery blanket in tow. I thought about how vulnerable she looked, her legs constrained by the bulky cloth nappy. Something between a duckling and a comedic sumo wrestler. I thought I should wash the blanket since it lived in her mouth. I thought about Henry, sighing because Ophelia had caught a stomach bug and couldn't go to nursery. I thought I must be a terrible mother.

'Mummy,' Ophelia mouthed, wrapping her chubby little arms around my leg.

'What did you say, honey?'

'Mummy,' she repeated, more confident this time.

'Yes, my love.' I picked her up and placed her on my lap, her blond hair glowing from the light of the computer screen. She looked angelic.

Emotion swelled inside my chest. I pulled her closer and lifted myself off the chair. 'That's right. Mummy's here.' For a long time, I rocked my hips side-to-side, standing in the middle of the room until her soft breathing told me she had fallen asleep. I carried her to her bedroom, deposited her gently amongst the army of cuddly toys guarding her from potential nightmares.

In the kitchen, I put the kettle on, took a mug from the cupboard, and placed a spoon of ground coffee into the French cafetière before reaching for the dictionary. I thumbed the pages; found the word I was searching for. *Integrity* – the quality or state of being complete or undivided. My mobile was on the breakfast counter. I pressed the last number and waited.

'Hello?'

'I came back too soon,' I blurted out, before Kerstin could say anything else.

'What about your piece?'

'Put it on ice. I'm not sure I'm ready for the truth.'

'Your choice,' Kerstin replied with a sigh.

When I hung up, I felt relieved.

The next morning, I walked Ophelia to nursery, then headed to the coffee shop. 'Oat latte, please. Two shots,' I told the barista behind the counter.

'Okay dokey,' he chimed with singing enthusiasm. 'You go find a seat. I'll bring it to you, love.'

I winced. Twenty years in the UK and I had never got used to the familiarity of this casual term of endearment. I found a seat at a little square table by the shop window, an ideal vantage point for people-watching. I lost myself in the ballet of morning commuters, specks floating in and out of my field of vision. In this neighbourhood, grey suits competed with pink turbans, yellow djellabas and multicoloured boubous. How many had come to the UK by choice, I wondered. A movement near my left shoulder brought me out of my reverie. The barista was standing there, smiling. He placed a lime-coloured mug on the table, pushing the jar of sugar cubes towards me.

'No notebook today, love?'

I couldn't tell if he was asking as part of an elaborate customer service routine or whether it was a genuine interest in his voice. 'No, not today,' I replied hurriedly. I was irritated by his sudden attention.

'The little girl kept you up all night?' he insisted.

What is this? I wondered. I repressed the urge to ask whether he should be manning the till. I watched as he crossed his arms against his chest, hugging the tray, obviously not going anywhere.

'I noticed a bit of an accent. Where' you from, love?'

I took a deep, slow breath, ready to give the little man my stock response.

'I was born in Paris, but I've lived here all my adult life, so this is home really.'

'Oh, I love Paris. I've always wanted to go.'

If I had a penny for every time…

'Thank you for the coffee anyway.' I picked up the mug, downed the bitter drink in one gulp, burning my tongue in the process. I replaced the mug on the table a bit too hard, swiped my bag, moved to stand. 'Time to go. Have a good day.'

'That was quick,' he commented. 'In a rush today?'

I nodded.

'Tomorrow, then?' he said, with puppy eyes.

'Yeah,' I replied with little conviction. I don't think so, I muttered to myself as I pushed the glass door and stepped into the street. Flustered, I walked aimlessly until I reached a small rose garden overlooking a manicured bowling green. I selected a secluded bench, hidden between two large bushes speckled with fragrant yellow flowers. From a safe distance, I watched dog walkers exchanging well-rehearsed morning greetings, Filipino nannies pushing rosy-cheeked toddlers on swings, suited office workers, noses in their smartphones. I could hear my heart pumping hard into my ears. A familiar sense of injustice at having been singled out yet again. Because I sounded different, people defined me as someone I had ceased to be two decades ago. No amount of time spent here would ever make any difference. Yet, back in France, life was going on without me. I felt in limbo. My life an oxymoron. The world kept passing me by.

It was great to watch Ophelia paddle in my in-laws' pool with her friends for her sixth birthday party. She would be starting Year

Two the following week. Back at the house the next morning, I made sure to iron her new school uniform before returning to my desk. Soon it would be my turn to return to work full-time. I put my fountain pen down on the green hardcover of the Moleskine notebook I carried around like a second brain, sipped some of the matte tea Henry had brought back from a stag weekend somewhere, rubbed my eyes with the flat of my palms. They had been feeling increasingly strained. It could be lack of sleep or middle age calling for reading glasses. When had I reached that kind of age, I wondered? I looked at the time. 10 o'clock. Women's Hour was on. I switched on the little digital radio that stood on the breakfast bar of our new three-bedroom house in the heart of Chelsea. Kerstin's familiar voice filled my kitchen.

'...Magazine X is a new brand of journalism. We want to bring back the long form – appeal to those readers who are looking for more depth.'

'So, tell us Kerstin, what can the readers expect from your first edition?'

'We've lined up great journalists to talk about issues that we feel passionate about and to bring the readers real stories from around the world. Every month we pick a topic and invite contributors from around the globe, trying to get as broad a perspective as possible.'

'What was the driving force behind your approach?'

'As the Editor-in-Chief, I'm keen for us to bring authentic voices to the reader. The world of literature is increasingly tackling the issue of appropriation, but Western journalism is still a long way away from this debate. We continue to put our own prism on international events. I don't believe this serves the reader. It creates biased information which has fed the rise of online, unmoderated

media, claiming to offer unaltered truth. This colonialist atti-tude has opened the gate to a sea of fake news. The readers were thirsty for raw information, but without the principles that drive good quality journalism, information can easily be manipulated. History has shown how dangerous that can be....'

The interview continued whilst I stared into my cup of yellow-ish tea. As Kerstin's voice trailed off, I picked up my discarded mobile from the counter, selected her name from my contact list and typed a congratulatory message, supplemented with two obligatory thumbs up. I pressed send, the message vanishing with a whoosh. I thought about what she had said. About how easy it had become to throw words into the ether. It reminded me of the beginning of a poem by Victor Hugo about the dangers of words, an exhortation not to throw them into the air without care.

I thought about letter-writing. Words traced on a page, carrying greater constancy, dependability, gravitas even. Hand-written words had always felt more serious, as if they denoted a more rigorous commitment. The virtual word, by contrast, felt frivolous by nature. Dangerous. Unsettling. *Panem et circenses* – bread and circuses. Entertainment, for the purpose of drowning the masses' good judgment. Kerstin was publicly stepping onto a battlefield, to counter the rise of fake news before *reliable* journalism was fully annihilated. A call for survival.

My phone vibrated on the breakfast bar, Kerstin's face flashing on the screen.

'So, what did you think?' she asked.

'Very relatable.'

'I'm glad you like it. I want you on the next edition, Iris.'

'Oh, Kerstin. I don't know. I'm only just coming back. I thought I'd start slow.'

'Nonsense. We need to get you back on the horse.'

'But I've been a recluse for almost seven years now. What would I possibly write about?'

'I have just the thing. Come by my office later.' She hung up. Leaving me frowning at her picture on the fading screen.

Half an hour later, I pushed the door of the new office near St Pancras station. The busy newsroom had been invaded by a handful of over-eager young people, dressed in brightly coloured dungarees, staring at shiny silver laptops covered in stickers. Across the room, I could see Kerstin, gesticulating through a glass-panelled wall at more dungareed kids gathered around a stand-up desk. As I pushed the glass door to get in, she waved at the school of eager interns, shouting instructions about the design cover.

'Grab a seat, sweetheart. Coffee?'

'I'm good, thanks. Tell me about that idea of yours then.'

Instead of responding, she slid a blue Post-it note across her stand-up bamboo desk.

'What's that?' I asked, aware of my involuntarily raised eyebrow.

'An address,' she replied, enigmatic.

I scrutinised the words scribbled on the little blue square.

'Well, I can see it's an address. And?'

'I want you to do an interview for me. This is the address.'

'In Paris?'

Kerstin handed me a large A4 envelope stamped with the magazine logo. 'Here. Eurostar ticket, Euros and a hotel booking. You're leaving in two hours.'

'But, Kerstin, I can't just...' Kerstin was staring at me in a way that said the discussion was over. 'I'll need to go home to grab my passport and arrange for someone to collect Ophelia from after-school class,' I replied, changing tack.

'Already taken care of,' she smiled. 'I spoke to your lovely other half.' She took something out of the drawer under her desk. 'Your passport. I know you're ready.'

'Henry gave you my passport? That's a conspiracy! Fine,' I said, raising my hands in surrender. 'And who exactly am I interviewing there?'

It had been years since my last Eurostar journey. The terminal at St Pancras International was new, modern, brought to life by rows of luxury shops, restaurants and cafés, more akin to an international airport terminal than a London train station. The walk from Magazine X's new headquarter only took seven minutes. It was almost fated.

At the Gare du Nord, I wavered between a taxi ride and the anonymity of the Metro, favouring the later. I emerged three quarters of an hour later onto Avenue Kleber, moving past the two-wheelers parked on the pavement, in front of two cafés busy with men in tailored suits, tourists and students in tight jeans and designer trainers. Patisserie Carette stood in between, timeless. This Paris institution had been a purveyor of fine macaroons since before I was born. I skirted around Café Kleber, towards the relative quiet of the tree-lined avenue where executive offices were interwoven with luxury apartments. A bank, a pharmacy, a couple of restaurants. Different names, same locations. First right, then left onto Rue de Lübeck and its succession of consulates and embassies. Tunisia. Kuwait. Around the corner, Bahrain. I was a stone's throw away from where Lady Diana had died. I stopped in front of the address from the Post-it note. Pressed a buzzer. A voice emerged from the bowels of the Haussmanian building. 'Come in.'

I stepped into the familiar corridor, leading to a carved wooden door in dark oak, out of place amongst the rows of bright posters adorning the walls. The brass sign confirmed this was still the school's main reception. Next to the door, a glass panel fitted with a communication grille revealed a small office filled with piles of paper, a lost property box overflowing with discarded jumpers, a football. In the middle, a thin woman with long limbs and grey eyes sat behind a patinaed school desk, impassive, absorbed in the transcription of written information into a large logbook. It was like stepping back in time. Lightly, I knocked on the glass, suddenly fearful to disturb her. She looked up.

'Can I help you?' she enquired in a gentle voice, refined to put visitors at ease.

I presented the piece of paper I had been clutching in my right hand since Kerstin's office. The woman turned a little brass handle to the right of the glass, and part of the window opened inward. 'Let me take a look,' she offered, reaching out.

I let go of the paper, watching her as she examined the inscription in blue writing.

'She will be in her office. Second door on the right,' she informed me with a soft movement of the chin, placing the small square firmly back in my hand, before shutting the window. I watched as she returned to her seat and resumed her activity as if our exchange had only happened in my mind. When I remembered to move, I turned in the direction she had indicated. The muffled sound of my footsteps on the waxed wooden floor conjured up memories of girls in tight trousers and stripy blue tops, competing for the attention of a handful of boys not long admitted into what had been a girls-only school. We had all been part of a homogeneous tribe, driven by our emerging hormones. I wondered what they had all become. It was the curse of the emigrant to lose touch with their own past.

I stopped in front of a door painted forest green, which stirred a long-forgotten memory. This used to be the Head's office. No visible sign now. I looked back over my shoulder to make sure. *Second door on the right.* I made a fist of my right hand, still holding on to the paper. I knocked three times.

'Come in,' a poised voice called.

I turned the handle and pushed open the door.

There she stood, amongst music sheets overflowing from every corner of the room. Red socks. Brown Birkenstocks. Blue jeans. A baggy woollen jumper, swallowing her frail body. The hint of a grey stubble hidden under a colourful batik-style scarf.

'Come in, come in.'

'Sister Agnès?'

The woman's grey eyes smiled with recognition. 'Iris? Is that really you?'

I nodded, the enormity of the encounter swelling into my chest, making breathing laborious.

'Your friend said you would be coming.' She moved closer, squinting. 'It's really you,' she said in disbelief, placing her hand onto my flushed cheek.

Her cold touch startled me, sending a shiver across my shoulders. I pressed my own hand, clammy with emotion, against the thin paper of her skin.

'I didn't know…' I blurted out. 'I never tried to find her.' As if her presence had released a valve deep inside me, tears flowed freely down my cheeks. Until that moment, I hadn't realised just how much my obsessive research had affected me.

'I've been here, my child. Waiting.' As she said it, she drew my face delicately towards hers, placing a long kiss on my forehead. She directed me towards a small brown sofa, tucked in a corner of the room, by a frosted window. She invited me to sit.

For a moment, I was back in the little boiler room, collecting a letter. Questions were colliding in my mind. Questions to which there might finally be an answer.

'I didn't think you would have become a nun,' was all I managed to say after a while.

She laughed a clear laugh.

'I'm sorry. I don't mean...'

'I know what you mean, my child... I travelled, many years. Eventually, He called me back here. Told me someone would come.'

I looked at her, incredulous. It had been a very long time since I had believed in miracles.

'He brought you here, didn't he?' she said, cocking her head. 'Your friend told me you had questions for me?'

The thought of Kerstin, grinning with satisfaction from behind her bamboo desk, brought me back to the purpose of my visit. 'Yes, sorry,' I said, straightening myself on the sofa, haphazardly drying my tears with the palms of both hands. 'I'm here about Victoria.'

A frown creased Sister Agnès's forehead.

'You know, the penfriend you gave me in year 10,' I added, realising how much time had passed. Unsure how much Kerstin had already shared.

'I remember,' Sister Agnès replied. 'As if it were yesterday.'

'Good... I... I don't suppose you know what became of her?' I felt a huge lump pressing against my chest as I spoke the words. 'Did... Did she make it?'

I held my breath whilst Sister Agnès considered the question.

'We'll come to that,' she replied after what felt like a minute.

The pressure against my lungs was building.

'Are you sure this is the answer you really need?' she asked.

My head started spinning. The air in the room was heavy. Sweat was soaking my armpits, creating damp patches on my shirt. Sister Agnès was facing me, impassive, scrutinising my every reaction.

'Ask me,' she encouraged, taking hold of my warm hand in her cold fingers once more. 'It's OK.'

I felt anger rising in my stomach, cutting through the dizziness. My eyes lingered on the brown carpet, littered with music sheets. I had come all this way for answers. She was doing this Jesuit thing of answering a question with another question. I felt myself shaking, then her cold fingers squeezed my hand. I looked up to find her contemplating my inner turmoil. She was not the enemy, I reminded myself, taking a deep breath, forming the words in my head. 'Why me?' I asked, almost in a whisper. 'Why did you pick me to become Victoria's penfriend?'

Sister Agnès explained that as a novice she had become involved with a number of NGOs doing work in East Africa, around the Great Lakes region. When the first reports of the extermination of Tutsis had come from her contacts, she had tried to raise awareness of the situation amongst the influential parents of children attending the school, hoping that some of them would be able to reach with their proverbial long arm to someone in the French Government, but the evening news had already offered a different story, reporting a conflict between two opposing tribes, breeding indifference.

'The School Head ordered me to let it go, concerned I was pestering generous donors,' Sister Agnès told me. 'The more urgent the situation became, the less the establishment wanted to know. I was horrified.'

Then Agnès received a phone call from her sister, a schoolteacher in Rwanda, who provided a first-hand account of the systematic massacre of men, women and children; the concerted effort to remove all foreigners, driving busloads of expats to Kigali airport in order to prevent external witnesses, and the exodus to neighbouring countries of victims fleeing the massacre and perpetrators, fleeing the advance of Paul Kagame's troops, under the protection of a very prominent French Army. On hearing this, Agnès felt rage at the general inertia of those who must have suspected, and the complicity of those who knew for certain. She even told me about a US Embassy official who ordered evacuation *before* the plane of the Rwandan President was shot down.

'I was vaguely aware that some of you children had parents working in government. I spent days trawling through school records, looking for someone I could reach out to. During that time, I prayed for guidance. The direct approach hadn't worked, so I decided that I needed to find a way to appeal to someone's humanity.'

'And that's when you approached my class?'

'Yes. Your father worked in Cooperation in the African section. I knew from your school record that you had previously had a penfriend. I spoke to my sister, and we came up with a plan.'

'What did you think this could possibly achieve?' I asked, bewildered.

'I… I don't know, Iris. I was young and naïve. I'm so sorry we dragged you into all this.'

'I was just a child. Do you have any idea what this did to me?'

I told her about the friendship, the letters, the silence, the slow realisation of what had actually happened in Rwanda and in the camps, in Zaïre.

'Do you know what they did to all those women?' I told her, trembling with rage.

'I know,' she replied, hanging her head. 'It was unforgivable.'

'I couldn't do anything! My dad couldn't do anything!'

'I know that now.'

I told her about the three hundred stamps, which for me encapsulated the enormity of our impotence whilst 800,000 people were murdered. We both sat in contemplative silence afterwards. Together, yet apart. I thought about her confession, the way she had tried to manipulate my father through me. I thought about guilt, and about motives. About my desire to please her. About that feeling of not knowing. About Ophelia.

'I was only a child,' I told her.

She pressed her lips hard, forming a thin blue line across her face.

'Agnès.' I said. 'I could never remember your name, you know. Maybe…'

She looked up.

'You were one of us. Not yet a sister,' I continued. 'You were only a child, too.' On saying this, I placed my hand on her forearm. 'We were all just children.'

She acquiesced.

'What is strange is that I remember clearly the day when you gave me the letter, but I have no recollection of you after that. Where did you go?'

Sister Agnès sighed. 'I left here,' she said. 'I went to get Victoria.'

'You mean… she's alive?'

I watched as the wrinkles on her face became animated by some internal turmoil.

'That isn't my story to tell,' she said finally.

On the Eurostar the following day, I watched the symmetrical fields slipping away until the train reached the tunnel and its thirty minutes underground. On the other side, the English countryside revealed itself as a patchwork of smaller fields delineated by ancient hedges, home to a wealth of pollinating insects and wild beasts claiming the land as their own. We only occupied the land for a fraction of time. We, the industrial West, sought to tame it with order, innovative machines, ground-breaking chemical advances, a harnessing of the landscape. In the end, we only revealed our own ignorance, depleting the land, poisoning our waters, threatening biodiversity. I considered the parallel with the impact those same countries had had on their former colonies – the arrogance they displayed, and the damage it continued to cause. It occurred to me that whatever my father did, or didn't do, it would have been the result of a misguided world view, a corruption of history by men playing with countries like children play with toys. Men who subsequently relinquished all responsibility, pointing the finger at the Tutsi rebels. I often wondered if they believed their own lies.

Sister Agnès had displayed genuine remorse. She had expiated her faults by devoting her life to the service of children. She wouldn't say much more than that. I dialled Kerstin's number.

'You're in the office?' I asked when she picked up.

'How did it go?' she enquired with suspicious nonchalance.

'All right,' I replied. 'I'll do it.'

'Good. Are you coming in?'

'Not yet. I'm heading home. A load of washing to do.' Before she could say anything, I ended the call, switching my phone to airplane mode.

At home, I found Henry feeding Ophelia a generous plate of fish fingers and chips. In the few years since I had begun my research we had grown further and further apart, as if the horrors

I unearthed drew a wedge between us. I resented the time Henry had got to spend with Ophelia whilst I buried myself in descriptions of mass graves and dental identifications.

'How was Paris?' he asked, wiping the tomato sauce off his lips to kiss my cheek. 'Did you find some answers?'

Was that why he had given Kerstin the passport? To fix me? I bent towards him and pressed my lips to his, closing my eyes in a gesture intended to silence.

'Hello, my love,' I said, taking a seat next to my daughter, pulling a plate towards me. 'Any left for Mummy?' She grinned a toothless grin.

'Look Mummy, I've lost two teeth today. Do you think the tooth fairy will bring me money?'

'Of course, sweetheart,' I told her, wondering what it meant that in France's popular folklore the fairy was replaced by a mouse. Same collector's role. Different currencies. The rest was a matter of conventions.

After dinner, I took Ophelia to the bathroom to brush her fragile teeth and put her pyjamas on.

'Mummy, will you tell me a story?' she asked once tucked under her duvet.

'Ok, my love.'

Once upon a time, the kingdom of the Mwami covered the whole of the known earth. The Mwami had three sons: Gatwa, Gahutu and Gatutsi. As he was coming to the end of his life, the Mwami called his three sons, whom he loved equally.

- I have a task for you my sons. You must climb to the tallest mountain in my kingdom and report what you can see.

- Yes father, the three sons replied.

- Before you go, I have something for you.

The Mwami took out three earthen jars containing milk from under his robe and placed them on the ground.

- These are for you, he told his sons. One jar each. Be back by nightfall.

The three sons picked up a jar each and started on their journey. They were young and fast. Soon they reached the base of the tallest mountain and started to ascend. It was a hot day, and the climb was steep. The youngest son, Gatwa, felt his tongue swell up, his throat constrict. Remembering the milk he was carrying, and frightened by death, he decided to quench his thirst, glad his father had thought to give him something to drink. Gahutu, the second son, marched frantically up the mountain, certain if he reached the top before his brothers he would be rewarded. The earthen jar was heavy, and with the heat Gahutu started to slow down. Looking over his shoulder, he saw the eldest son, Gatutsi, on his heels. Stupid jar he thought, considering his burden. Thinking himself cunning, he spilled the content of the jar onto the mountain path. His jar much lighter, Gahutu reached the summit before Gatutsi. The eldest son, holding on to his jar, looked at the vast expense of earth and sky, taking in the lush and green land as far as the eye could see, the grazing cattle, the men, women and children working the fields.

– I beat you, brother, Gahutu boasted.

– Our journey is not complete, little brother. Father said to return by nightfall, Gatutsi replied with a smile.

And with that, he started down the slope, giving little Gatwa encouragement as he passed him.

By nightfall, all three sons had returned.

At their father's request, they placed their jar in front of them.

The Mwami stood and approached his youngest.

– Gatwa, my son, what did you see when you reached the top?

– The sky, father. The sky and the land. Your land.

Looking inside the empty jar, the Mwami asked his son what had happened to the milk.

– I drank it father, Gatwa replied. It was such a hot day.

The Mwami nodded, thanked his youngest and called his second son.

– What did you see when you reached the top Gahutu?

– My brothers' heads. I was first to reach the top, father.

The Mwami leaned forward to take a look at Gahutu's jar.

– And what of the milk? he asked.

– The jar was too heavy, father. It was slowing me down. I spilled the milk onto the path.

– I see, the Mwami replied.

Thanking his second son, he called his eldest, Gatutsi.

– What did you see when you reached the top my son?

– Your subjects, father; our people; the land which feeds men and cattle; the cattle which provide the milk.

The three sons obediently stood in front of their father. The Mwami uncovered the third jar, revealing thick, creamy milk. He nodded with contentment.

And it is said that on this day, the Mwami entrusted Gatutsi to command the others, and to guard the land, the cattle and all of the people.

I stood in the dark, listening to the soft noises of Ophelia's peaceful sleep. I remembered reading this parable to her when she was a baby. I had found a version of it in one of the books trying to make sense of what had led to the genocide. Hutu, Tutsi, Twa. Fairy. Mouse. All conventions created for convenience. All stories open to interpretation. When I had first read this parable, I had seen three siblings. Three equals. A reminder that it was Belgium's decision to include those descriptors on Rwandan identity cards, to single out the Tutsi as the ruling ethnic group, leading to resentment from the majority Hutu population, forging a platform on which the government would for sixty years build a narrative of 'them and us', slowly dehumanising the Tutsi, making them into the usurper. A borrowed narrative, aiding and abetting racism, to divide and rule. Sister Agnès was right. It wasn't our story to tell.

I walked to the bathroom and emptied the contents of the washing basket into a large plastic bag, walked back to the kitchen where Henry was setting the breakfast table.

'I'm going to the launderette,' I told him.

'Is something wrong with the washing machine?' he asked.

'I... It isn't going to do the job,' I replied.

Outside, I took the first left and walked twenty minutes in the direction of the address Sister Agnès had given me, looking for the laundromat sign. I found it, a few doors down from a kebab bar, illuminating the street with its neon green glow.

Victoria

The air hostess gently presses my left arm. 'Miss, we've landed,' she announces as I open my eyes.

I look around in a daze. The plastic shutter of the aeroplane window is down, preventing me from seeing outside. Close to me is a heap of grey blankets lit up by a single bulb set into the box above my head. Paul, safely wrapped up, has fallen asleep on the middle seat. Next to him is the woman with wild curly hair who met us a few hours before in Uganda. The sister's sister. She is smiling encouragingly in my direction. Her name is Agnès, like the lamb of God.

'How are you?' she mouths silently.

I smile a tight smile. She takes it as a signal to start gathering our meagre belongings. In the meantime, I brush the top of Paul's head, wary not to startle him. He bristles, unfolds himself like a stretching kitten, yawning wildly.

'We are here Paul.' Wherever *here* is, I think.

The plane jerks. Behind us, I hear a father explaining to his son that the pilot has released the landing gear. We are about to touch the ground, he tells him. I take hold of Paul's small hand in mine and pin him down to the armrest.

'Straighten your seat, close your table and open the shutters,' advises the voice of the hostess through the speakers before she takes her position at the end of the corridor. I look through the little round window, but outside is grey with thick clouds. I turn towards Paul, his face undecipherable. I think we are falling. For a moment, I imagine my brother lying on the ground, arms and legs torn from his body. Then we make contact with the tarmac, like a gymnast landing heavily after a long jump. The air hostess unclasps her safety belt and stands to make a final announcement, whilst I let go of the air trapped inside my lungs. We are to remain seated whilst the plane taxies us to the arrival lounge. Finally, the plane comes to a standstill. We are ready to move, shuffling down the aisle in a clumsy procession of ungainly limbs. At the door of the plane, an impeccably dressed pilot greets us. 'Thank you for flying with us,' he says with a competent smile. 'Enjoy your trip!'

I feel myself grimacing. Ahead of me is a telescopic corridor made of corrugated grey metal attached to the side of the plane. As I step onto it, it wobbles, as if it might detach itself. I turn towards the smiling pilot in panic. 'This way,' he directs, as if to be swallowed by a giant metal snake was the most natural thing in the world. Then I feel someone grabbing my hand. Agnès takes a step onto the corrugated floor, standing between Paul and me, holding both our hands. 'Come on, children,' she encourages. And with that, she takes another step, dragging us enthusiastically behind her.

The vibration from the floor tells me that Paul has picked up the pace and is now running alongside her to keep up. Trying to be brave, I lengthen my stride, so that by the time we reach the glass sliding gates at the end of the metal snake, the three of us form a unified front. The doors slide open onto a brightly lit corridor decorated with TV monitors and multicoloured posters welcoming us to Paris Charles de Gaulle.

'Are we really in Paris?' I ask, incredulous.

Before Agnès can answer, a woman's voice on a loudspeaker announces that all passengers from Entebbe International Airport are to attend gate three to retrieve their luggage.

'Passengers in transit to gate five,' the voice bellows in French, repeating the same instructions in English and another language I do not recognise.

'Gate five, that's us,' Agnès says. 'Come on.'

'Are we not staying?' I ask, staring at her with widening eyes. I mean Paris. I have a friend in Paris. She crouches down between us, looking serious.

'We have to go through customs now. Let me do the talking, OK?'

We both nod. She stands and leads us towards another brightly lit corridor, to a set of mechanical steps. Paul looks frightened for a second, but as soon as he steps onto the moving escalator, a grin of delight crosses his face. 'Look Victoria,' he says, laughing. 'I'm not even walking!'

It is good to hear his voice and to see him smile. There is hope, I think. Once we reach the next floor up, we find a large number of people dressed in colourful habits, grey suits and shorts and t-shirts, queuing in front of a giant blue sign covered in little flags and yellow lettering. Ahead of us, the queue seems to split into three lanes of different lengths. Under the little blue flag with yellow stars, the grey suits and shorts and t-shirts people seem to move quickly towards a row of glazed cabins. To the right of that lane are two longer, more colourful lines. I look at the sign above. It says *Non-EU. Others*. Sister Agnès pulls us towards the queue furthest to the right. The human line moves slowly, as people shuffle their hand luggage in front of them. To our left, the other lane is empty now. Finally, we reach a woman in a dark blue uniform who seems to direct people towards one of two cabins. I am alarmed at the sight of the gun attached to her belt. I stand very still, pressing my tongue against the roof of my mouth.

'One at a time,' the dark-uniformed woman says. 'Have your passport ready.'

Agnès leans towards her and whispers something so that people in the queue behind us cannot hear.

'Right, I see,' the uniformed woman replies loudly, eyeing Paul and me suspiciously. 'Wait here a moment.'

Behind us, the queue bristles with discontent, but nobody speaks. This is not the place to stand out, I think. We all understand this instinctively. The uniformed woman disappears behind a metal door armed with a keypad lock, reappearing a few minutes later, flanked with a tall grey man in identical uniform, armed with a clipboard.

'Follow me,' the grey man orders, raising an eyebrow at the sight of Paul's bare feet.

We do as he says, and he takes us into a windowless room furnished with a steel table and four orange plastic chairs. Directing us to sit, he turns towards Agnès.

'Papers,' he says.

She fishes something out of the front pocket of her backpack and hands him a slightly crumpled piece of paper, folded in four.

'Passports?' he asks.

'Only mine,' she explains handing him a small booklet with golden lettering with a trembling hand, before launching into a tentative explanation. 'The children are war refugees, you understand. They were forced to flee their home. They have lost all their belongings.'

She looks too nervous.

'Parents?' the man asks, without looking up from his clipboard.

'It's all on the form… They're war orphans… We have permission…'

As she says it, I think that if I don't believe her the man probably won't either. A pressure on my chest radiates as I wonder what these armed people will do to us.

'We'll see,' the man eventually replies, noting something down and handing her passport back. 'They'll have to stay overnight, until we can clear this up. You can go.'

'I'm not leaving them. They're in my care,' she replies, her voice steadier now.

'Look, Miss, you can't stay here. You're a French citizen, your passport is in order; you have to go.'

'But…what about them?' she asks, desperation in her voice. 'We have a flight to catch.'

'Not tonight, you don't.' Lifting his gaze to meet hers, he softens a little. 'Relations between France and the UK are tense when it comes to refugees. I've been asked to make sure we double-check all applications before people leave the Schengen area. Only doing my job, Miss.'

'I understand,' she concedes.

I don't. She brought us all this way, to Paris. And now she is going to leave us with this man? She must have seen the incomprehension in my eyes. She turns one of the orange chairs towards me, sits and lifts Paul onto her lap. 'Victoria, you are going to have to be brave. This man is going to take care of you until tomorrow, then we'll continue our journey. Yes?' We both nod in unison, uncertain what else we can do. She looks up towards the official. 'Can I have your name please? And assurance that you will take care of these children personally until this is all cleared up? Believe me, they've been through enough already.' My eyes are moving from her face to the man's gun and back, half expecting him to draw his weapon and shoot her in the face.

After an endless silence, the man acquiesces, hands her his name on a piece of paper and promises we will be well cared for. 'I'll ring you tomorrow,' he says.

She draws us to her chest, kissing our cheeks, promising to be back the next morning. 'Be good, you hear? For me.'

Is she abandoning us? I wonder. Paul is looking at me with a deep frown. I remind myself I have to be strong. For him. Behind us, the voice of the man with the clipboard is saying something.

'Are you kids hungry?' he asks in a softer tone.

Paul looks at me for a cue. The man moves closer to us. As he does, the smell of cologne fills my nostrils. Celine's dad used to wear cologne. I decide that we can trust this man who does not carry the stench of death. I wrap my arm over Paul's shoulders, and we follow the man out.

I lie on soft cotton sheets that night, staring at the ceiling. Earlier, Paul and I were taken to a noisy refectory where people in colourful dresses and shirts from all over the world ate a meal of pilau rice and fish, and ice cream for the children. Afterwards, the grey man brought us to this little room with two single beds standing against opposite walls, a small table between them. In the absence of windows, I have lost track of time. It was morning when we arrived. It feels late now. Content with a warm meal, Paul has dropped asleep and is gently snoring. I wonder whether his constant sleeping is a sign that he is starting to heal somehow, or whether he is slowly drifting away. So much has happened. I realise I have no idea what month it is. Time ceased to flow once we got to the camp, and our current situation seems to defy reality. I think about Data, in pain, in the hut on the edge of lake Kivu. I think about what it means that we are now imprisoned in France. It feels absurd to have come all this way to be locked up, but Paul and I could neither stay in Zaïre nor return to Rwanda. All we could do was run. Now that we have stopped, in this grey metal box, waiting for someone else to decide on our fate, I feel a great emptiness. I try to bring up the faces of those we left behind, but they are evading me already. I call their names out loud: 'Celine, Mama, Data.' Maybe if I call their names every night, their spirits will watch over us, Paul and me. It is just the two of us now.

That night is the first night I have the dream.

I am back in school in Rwanda, playing under the tree. I hear someone calling my name in the distance. I turn. Celine is standing halfway between the tree and our classroom, waving at me. She is calling my name. I wave back, gesturing her to join me under our tree. She starts running, but the more she runs the further away she seems to be, until Benjamin appears between us. She is running with fear in her eyes now. I go to reach her, but she is too far away. I watch, powerless, as Benjamin strikes her to the ground. He is wearing big leather boots, like the ones white officers wore in the films about World War Two they showed us in school. He raises his foot, landing a blow on Celine's head. I hear the sound of her crushed skull. I press my hands over my ears and scream.

When I wake, the bedsheets are soaked in my own sweat, my blue dress creased and twisted around my body. In my head, the screaming and the crushing sound resonate for what feels like hours. The chill of death wraps me in its grip, sending shivers down my spine, until all that is left is darkness. By the time I wake again, I am in a different bed. Paul is quietly sitting on a large blue plastic chair, colouring the shape of a tortoise in a colouring book. Agnès is standing by my side. She explains that the immigration officers found me on the floor of our cell in the morning, teeth chattering, delirious. I have been taken into hospital for observation since it appears that I have developed a fever.

'Paul will be staying with me until you're better,' she tells me, her voice gentle. 'The doctor says it should only take a few days.'

'No,' I say, weakly. 'You can't take Paul too.'

'It's only for a few days, Victoria.'

She explains that the doctor assumed I had cholera or dysentery at first, since we have come from a refugee camp. Now the doctor thinks my body might be in shock from delayed trauma.

'Paul stays with me,' I tell her with feeble authority.

'Be reasonable. He'll be with me and we'll come back tomorrow.'

'Then what?' I ask.

'The French government won't allow you to stay without a sponsor—'

'But I have a friend in Paris. Someone with whom Paul and I can stay…'

Before I can finish, she continues, 'I've spoken to friends who work for a charity helping East African refugees. As soon as you're better, I'll take you to them.'

'Take us? Where?'

'London.'

'London? But why? Find Iris. Find my friend. She can be our sponsor.'

'Only adults can be sponsors, Victoria. Be reasonable.'

That is the second time she urges me to be reasonable. 'Is there something you're not telling me?'

'I… I approached Iris's parents. They're not willing to sponsor you… I'm sorry Victoria.'

I don't understand. 'Leave me,' I tell her.

I watch as she packs the coloured pencils Paul has been using, helps him put on a red coat I have never seen before, and invites him to follow her. As they disappear down the corridor, I notice Paul is wearing socks and a pair of matching red trainers.

In the end, it takes me another two weeks to recover. On top of the general exhaustion, I contracted the flu. My stay in hospital is strange. Twice a day, someone comes to take my temperature and administer colourful pills which the nurse promised are going to make me better. Three times a day, someone brings warm food on a trolley. Soup at first, as I am too weak to digest anything else, then cooked meals, salad, deserts. I have yoghurt for the first time in my life. I wonder what Mama would have thought of someone bringing food on wheels. The rest of the time, the nurses bring me orange juice and sugary tea. They tell me it is to make me strong again, but I get the impression I am getting special treatment. One of the nurses is from East Africa. She brings chocolate once.

On the day of my release, Paul and Agnès come early to pick me up. She has brought me warmer clothes: a pair of jeans, a bright yellow shirt and a thick woollen cardigan.

'She made this for you,' Paul informs me. 'It's called *knitting,*' he adds with a self-important grin.

Agnès laughs as I thank her. 'It's nothing. London will be cold.'

She also brought me some yellow socks and a pair of dark blue trainers. She helps me put on the socks, since it is my first time manoeuvring those over my heel. They feel tight and itchy. As we are about to leave, she hands me a heavy coat with a large hood and funny looking buttons which remind me of goat hooves. 'A duffel coat,' she tells me.

Coming out of the hospital, the cold air punches the breath out of my lungs. I have never felt so cold. A fine drizzle of rain deposits tiny droplets onto the felted wool of my coat sleeve. Around us, the air is a pale blue. Tall buildings across the road block the light, making everything seem muted. Agnès pushes me into a black car. Inside the taxi, there is a strong smell of leather, mixed with cold cigarette smoke. 'To the airport,' she says.

The driver is middle-aged, chatty. He came from Cameroon with his parents when he was very young. Now he has his own family. Three boys. He points at a picture in a small plastic frame hanging from his rear-view mirror. Sister Agnès congratulates him on his beautiful family.

'Family is everything,' he replies. I feel a jolt, check on Paul. He seems oblivious, lost in the developing landscape of skyscrapers rushing past the car window. The volume of traffic is overwhelming. I think about the way Iris once described Paris to me. *Big, white and shiny.* All I see is grey, grey, grey.

Finally, we reach the airport. Agnès assures us that all the paperwork is in order this time, but as we reach the security gate, I see soldiers in full battle gear, carrying huge machine guns. My throat tightens. Everything goes fuzzy. All I can hear is the sound of crushed skulls echoing in my head. I am half conscious of my body dropping to the ground.

'Victoria, Victoria.' Agnès's voice reaches me through a fog.

I blink, her face suddenly in front of me. Paul's face appears next to hers. 'It's OK, Sis', he tells me.

Slowly, I rise to my feet, leaning on Agnès. Paul is holding onto my forearm.

'Wait a moment,' Agnès says. She walks towards a rotund British Border patrol guard with a friendly demeanour and murmurs something to her. Her hair is wrapped in a bright scarf decorated with hibiscus flowers which contrast with her severe uniform. 'What's your name, sweetheart?' she asks in a motherly voice.

'…Victoria…' I manage. 'My name is Victoria.'

'Well, Victoria, you remind me of my daughter.' She smiles. 'Agnès here tells me you have to catch a flight to London. Have you ever been to London?' As she asks, she takes my arm and directs me towards the security gate.

'No. Never been to London,' I whisper between ragged breaths.

'Ah!' she exclaims. 'You don't want to be late, then. There's a lot to visit in London.'

I manage a grin.

'Lots of museums and lovely buildings. But most of all, lots of lovely parks. So many green parks with wild ducks and swans floating about on artificial lakes. Have you ever seen a swan?'

I admit I haven't. We continue to walk, still chatting.

'Swans are huge white birds.'

'Do people eat them?' I ask.

'Ah, no, sweetheart. They belong to the Queen of England, you see.' As she says it, she hands my paper to her colleague in the booth. The colleague glances at the papers and returns them to us. The woman with the colourful headwear turns to Agnès. 'Here you go, all set.' And to me, 'Have a wonderful journey Victoria. You have the name of a great queen.'

As we wait to board the plane, I ask Agnès about the woman's singing accent.

'Jamaica. Many people from Jamaica moved to England in the 1950s and 1960s,' she tells me.

I feel encouraged by the thought.

We spend our first night in England in a strange place. It is neither a hotel, nor someone's home. Agnès tells us we are in a Bed & Breakfast, and I guess that is exactly what it is. We are given a room for the night, Paul and I together. Agnès is next door. Our room smells of lavender, dust and mould. Everyone is sharing a bathroom with a huge bath on golden claws like something out of a Hollywood movie.

In the morning, I watch as a wrinkled white lady with silver-white hair pours black tea from an intricate flowery pot with a spout shaped like a beak into a delicate china cup with the thinnest of handles, balanced on a matching saucer. Putting down the teapot, she indicates a jug from the same set.

'White, dear?'

'I…. I'm not sure…' I have no idea what she is asking.

'Do you take your tea milky?' she clarifies with a forgiving smile.

'I don't know. I mean, I've never tried.'

Agnès interrupts her conversation with the bespectacled man who joined us for breakfast and turns to me. 'I'd have the milk,' she advises. 'They make their tea really strong here. It's undrinkable otherwise.'

'Builders' tea,' the old woman nods proudly. 'Quality. From Kenya,' she adds, as if this fact should mean something to me.

She takes the jug and adds its thick yellowy content to the little cup, turning the liquid from dark amber to insipid beige. I thank her with a smile, wondering why anyone would want to drink something that colour, but I am grateful for the squares of toasted white bread smothered in butter and raspberry conserve.

Next to me, Paul is staring intently at a small bowl overflowing with little white and brown cubes. Catching his gaze, the old woman giggles. 'Bit of a sweet tooth, lad?' She points at the bowl. 'Take as many as you want. They're yours.'

Paul's eyes widen and he snatches a little brown cube balancing on the edge of the bowl. He deposits his loot on the tip of his tongue, carefully closes his mouth and starts crunching, eyes closed like a cat.

'You'll have to brush your teeth well after that,' Agnès warns him. 'People use sugar cubes to sweeten their tea,' she says in response to my inquisitive gaze.

I grab a little white cube and drop it into the beige beverage. The sugar disappears, submerged in the opaque liquid. Picking up the cup, I give it a little swirl and take a sip of the strange mixture. Bitter, creamy and sweet. I take another sip, the warmth spreading down my throat and into my stomach, giving a strangely comforting sensation.

'I like it,' I tell Agnès. From the door, the old woman is smiling.

A young man from the charity Agnès mentioned to us in Paris has come to meet us. I notice he is wearing old trainers caked in mud.

'Basically, because they're unaccompanied minors, an adult needs to be appointed as guardian,' he tells Agnès, adding that the process will take time, which is tricky since, as asylum seekers – apparently that is what we are – we are not allowed to work, nor can we claim something he calls *benefits*. 'The easiest solution would be for you to become their guardian,' he whispers to Agnès.

He claims to be a solicitor, but I find it hard to believe. Agnès nods. Data always wore ironed shirts and polished leather shoes to work. Data. The image of his torn clothes and dirty bandage flashes back into my mind. I wonder where he is now. As far as I know, I am now the head of our family.

'I can take care of Paul,' I say.

'It's OK, Victoria. You don't have to.' Agnès tells me, placing her hand on my forearm.

'I want to,' I insist. I turn to the man. 'Tell me how.'

'Well, since she's sixteen, we can apply for Victoria to become an emancipated minor,' he says, more to Agnès than to me.

I feel anger rising in my stomach. 'I'm here,' I tell him. 'Talk to me.'

I realise I must have raised my voice as Paul's head jerks up to check what is happening. By the door to the dining room, I see the old woman is staring too.

'Sorry,' he says, appeasing. 'You are my client, of course, and I will do as you instruct, but I would advise you to find a guardian as it might make things simpler in the short term.'

'I could stay,' Agnès offers. 'Until you're settled.'

I try to stuff the anger back inside me. These people are trying to help, I remind myself. But what do they know? Next to me, I catch a glimpse of Paul trying to sneak another sugar cube into his mouth. Agnès spots him too. We exchange an amused glance. This is about taking care of Paul.

'Ok,' I tell the man. 'So, what do we do next?'

In the end, Agnès offers to stay with us for two years as our guardian, to give me a chance to finish school, and to help set up what she calls appropriate care for Paul and me.

The man turns out to be a real solicitor, and a pretty good one too. We are granted indefinite leave to remain in the UK. This comes with the right to work. Agnès writes a letter to her convent school in Paris, delaying her vows. With the help of the charity, we find a small flat above a launderette. Paul is enrolled in a local primary school and I go to Sixth Form College. Agnès finds a job packing and delivering vegetables in a local grocery store, and volunteers for the charity that helped to bring us here.

I know she receives news from her sister who went back to Rwanda after the government of Paul Kagame took power. It is hard to get a sense of what is happening there since the BBC presents a narrow view of the world which largely excludes the African continent. Through the charity, though, we learn that people have been arrested and that the jails are so full it would take several generations to prosecute everyone that was involved in the killings. An International Tribunal has been set up and the key architects of the genocide have been incarcerated – amongst them, the Colonel. I wonder whether the documents Data smuggled ever made it to their destination. Agnès says the Colonel is the first man in history to plead guilty to the crime of genocide. We never talk about it, but I am certain someone from the charity is trying to locate Benjamin.

When it is time to attend the first Parents' Evening at Paul's school, Agnès and I go together. I am startled by the rows of desks behind which teachers sit. One table, two chairs. One table, two chairs. One table... Agnès pulls at my sleeve, and we cross the large wood-panelled hall under the scrutiny of women with straightened blond hair and tight-fitting jeans, with impeccably suited husbands like accessories; nurses in their blue uniforms with small round watches pinned to their front; postmen in shorts and orange high-vis jackets; turbaned men, women in saris; the odd tracksuit combo. We must look like an intriguing pair, even amongst this diverse slice of humanity. A young man with a rainbow badge pinned to his rucksack gives me the thumbs up. A lanky ginger boy dressed in the school uniform approaches us. 'Which class?' he asks drily.

'Year three,' Agnès replies.

He indicates two red plastic chairs. 'Wait there,' he says. 'The teacher will call you.'

Looking at this boy of about eleven inflated with the importance of his task, I think that not so long ago this would have been me. I remember how eagerly Celine and I volunteered to help the sisters. Always the reliable ones. I remember how we painted flags on the school wall to welcome the committee that day. Celine's bloody face flashes in front of my eyes; my knee buckles. I waver, try to hold on to something, collapse onto a set of parents waiting on identical red plastic chairs. *I hear the sound of skulls being crushed.*

When I come round, Agnès is bent over me, holding a plastic cup filled with water. 'Drink this,' she says, helping me up. Around us, the bustle of the Assembly Hall has receded. All eyes are on me, in that self-conscious way people look, pretending they are not really looking. I feel my cheeks burning.

'What happened?' someone asks.

'It's nothing. Probably the heat,' Agnès says, helping me to my feet and walking me to our allocated plastic chairs. 'Are you OK?' she asks quietly as we sit down.

'I think so. It's being back in a school hall…' My voice trails off.

'I understand,' she says, wrapping her hands over mine.

After a few minutes, the low vibration of blended conversations between parents and teachers fills the room once more, once again immersing us in guarded anonymity. Another few minutes, and the teacher calls Paul's name. Agnès and I stand in unison. We make our way towards the table and are invited to perch on tiny plastic chairs intended, I'm convinced, to dwarf us compared to the teacher.

'Are you Paul's parents?' she asks in the diplomatic tone of the politically correct – culturally aware, yet not certain quite what we are.

'Victoria is Paul's older sister,' Agnès explains. 'I'm their guardian.'

The teacher lets out a sigh then, as if preparing to take on the impossible task she has been set. After all, she has been put in charge of the well-being of a class of thirty disparate eight-year-olds with a multiplicity of conflicting needs.

'Paul is a lovely boy,' she starts, before adding that despite the counselling and additional educational support he has received, he is struggling both educationally and socially. 'He has difficulties playing nicely with the other children...' she pauses, staring at the notes in front of her. '...which is understandable considering his circumstances.'

'What do you mean, *difficulties*?' Agnès asks, straightening herself on the tiny chair.

'Well, Paul has a tendency to react with great violence... and I can imagine why, but you have to appreciate we have a duty of care towards the other children in the class,' she whispers to us, before clamping her jaw shut.

How can you possibly imagine? I think.

'What do you mean, violent?' I say out loud, steadying my voice. 'Paul has always been the gentlest of boys.' As I say it, I remember the sound of the panga slicing through Benjamin's flesh and my heart sinks.

'Is there anything more you can do?' Agnès asks. 'Any further support you can offer?'

The teacher seems to deflate with relief. Some parents must scream at her on those evenings. For the first time, I take stock of the woman in front of us. She is petite, blonde and freckled, dressed in a black cotton dress covered in tiny daisies, buttoned at the front like a man's shirt. There are remnants of blue paint under her nails and she wears a necklace the children clearly made for her out of decorated bottle caps. I can tell she is a good person trying her best. I remember my own children in the camp and the drawings they made to brighten our situation.

'We would really appreciate your help,' I tell her.

'How are your A levels going?' she asks. I realise that, to her, I am just a teenage girl who has come with her guardian.

'Fine, yes. Is there anything more we can do to help Paul?' I insist, taking a deep breath. 'When I was teaching in the camp, we found that children who had witnessed their relatives being exterminated experienced a range of complex emotions.' I pause, my voice trembling.

The teacher, Mrs Jones, cocks her head to one side, observing me with a mixture of pity and surprise. 'Of course,' she says.

'What Victoria is trying to say, is that Paul has experienced unimaginable trauma at the hands of his own people.' Agnès speaks quickly, her words staccato. 'We appreciate that it's difficult for his schoolmates to relate, but Paul is not a bad person. He just needs time in a nurturing environment.'

'I understand,' Mrs Jones replies, averting her eyes. 'In truth, I don't think our school counsellor is best qualified to provide Paul with the kind of support that we think he needs, but I'm happy to work with you to see if we can find a specialist school that can provide him with additional support.' She makes a note in her file. 'I'll be in touch. Thank you for coming today. It's useful to meet families to get a better sense of our children.'

As she reverts to the formulaic phrase she must use to dismiss all parents, I try to weigh the implications of what she has just said. As I do, I am vaguely aware of Agnès thanking her and dragging me away.

'What does this mean?' I ask her when we are back outside, walking towards our little flat.

'It means that the School Board of Trustees decided that Paul is no longer welcome in that school,' she replies stoically. 'I don't think there's any point challenging their decision,' she adds.

In my mind, Paul is still a sweet little seven-year-old boy dribbling his football in the back garden with wide smiling eyes. We came all this way for a chance at a normal life, running away from the fate that awaited us in the camp. The charity arranged sessions with a specialist to help us 'work through' what we experienced; we forged a new normal for ourselves...

'Were we too late?' I ask Agnès as we cross the road in front of the laundromat.

'Oh, Victoria. No. Of course not.' She takes hold of my forearm. 'We'll find the right place for him.'

As I look up, I see the strain on Agnès's face. I know in that moment that she is doubting her own words.

'Victoria?' The voice of Agnès on the other end of the receiver seems strangely far away. After I passed my A levels, she stayed to help out with Paul whilst I took an evening class to become a primary school teacher. After that, she returned to Paris and took her vows, becoming a missionary nun like her sister. I now work three days a week as a teaching assistant, ironically at the school that failed to retain Paul. The rest of the time, I take care of my little brother. After many meetings with the Local Education Authority, it became obvious nobody wanted the responsibility of a child with this degree of 'unpredictable aggressivity', as his file described it. One of the Liaison Officers suggested home schooling.

For three years, I taught him with the support of two volunteers from the charity. Our efforts paid off, and he was readmitted into mainstream education in Year Seven. This year, Paul is taking his A levels.

'Victoria, they've located Benjamin.' On hearing his name, I am dizzied by a raft of conflicting emotions. For years now, charity volunteers in Rwanda have been cataloguing victims and perpetrators, in an attempt to reunite families and give people closure. Counselling taught me to weigh what Benjamin has done against the possibility of forgiving. He was a child, manipulated by bad people, the counsellor reminded me. Today, I want to believe that part of the little brother I knew has survived; that somehow we can all be reunited, one day. After all, my efforts with Paul seem to have paid off. He is well adjusted now. No longer fuelled by blind rage.

'Where is he, Agnès?'

'He's in a Rwandan rehabilitation centre. He was too young to face trial.'

I have read about the Rwandan government's attempt to expedite cases by reviving the ancient custom of the *Gacaca* court. It started in 2001, maybe to feed the ongoing rumbles of a wounded population looking for answers. Perpetrators, accused by witnessing survivors, expiate their sins in front of specially elected judges – *inyangamugayo*. After atonement comes forgiveness for the accused, and the promise of closure for the victims' families. I assumed Benjamin would be one of those people.

'Does this mean Benjamin could be released?' At the thought of this, fear suddenly takes hold of me. I fear for Paul. He has come so far, but his mind is a fragile ecosystem that could be overthrown by the news of Benjamin's freedom. For years Paul experienced nightmares, his older brother chasing him, stump bleeding, the panga raised in his remaining hand. I fear for us too. Would Benjamin seek retribution for our perceived betrayal, for the loss of his hand?

'It's a possibility. What do you want me to tell them, the charity people?'

I realise Agnès is asking if I want them to put us in contact.

'I don't know, Agnès. Can I think about it?'

'Of course. I don't think the rehabilitation centre will release him for a while.'

All night I toss and turn, unable to silence the thoughts churning inside my mind. A decade is a long time. Our life is not the one we left behind. Paul has a chance at a good future. I have a chance, even if sometimes I feel that I died on the edge of lake Kivu. Mama. Data. Celine. All those ghosts pursue me night after night. But Benjamin is our flesh and blood. Family. Our only surviving relative. If there is even a slim chance that part of my little brother still exists in this young man awaiting to start afresh, do I not owe it to him to reach out? I remember talking with the sister about forgiveness when we were still in the camp.

'Anger is the devil's greatest tool,' she said. 'It will consume you until you lose yourself.'

Forgiveness, then. Not for his sake but for mine.

Before I know it, it is morning, and I am setting up the breakfast table. From the bathroom, I hear the sound of the electric razor which marks the beginning of Paul's day.

'Morning, Sis,' he calls, coming to stand beside me as I fry a pan of fried eggs and bacon. He kisses the top of my head, his way of reminding me that I am the little one now, before sitting at the kitchen table and pouring us both a cup of white tea. He takes his with three sugars. I recall his delight at the sugar cube when we first arrived all those years ago. We eat in silence, listening to the morning news on BBC Radio 4. I observe the chiselled face of the young man who has grown under my care. His face is handsome, bearing no visible marks of the horror his beautiful eyes once witnessed. He looks the regular teenager, less moody than some of his school mates. He gave up playing football after we arrived in the land of Liverpool FC and Manchester United. Instead, he has the broad shoulders of a competitive swimmer and I have shelves full of trophies. His achievements make me proud.

'Can I ask you something, Paul?'

'Sure,' he replies, chewing on a piece of bacon.

'Would you ever want to go back?'

'Go back where?'

'Home…Rwanda.'

His face falls still. He places his fork on the edge of the plate as if in slow motion. I notice the thumping of a vein along his left temple, his eyes scrutinising mine. The air takes on the consistency of thick marmalade. I want to hold my breath and make myself minuscule. We remain like that, fixed, for a whole minute.

'This is home, Sis,' he says finally.

Wiping the corner of his mouth with the back of his hand, he picks up a pile of school textbooks and folders and stuffs them into his rucksack.

'Got to go!' he says. The front door slams shut before I can reply, the vibration sending a jolt to my heart. I recognise the familiar grip on my insides. I have felt this sort of fear before.

An hour passes whilst I try to make sense of what just happened. In the end, I rise to pick up the phone and ring Agnès in Paris. 'Could they arrange for someone to pass on a letter to Benjamin?'

'I believe so,' she replies.

Over the next few months, I have several conversations with the counsellor about the decision to keep Benjamin's whereabouts from Paul. I tell her it is to protect Paul, that it took him a long time to exorcise his own demons and that bringing Benjamin into his life now could destabilise him at a crucial time in his education. I tell myself it is better not to bring back the memory of what happened in the camp. In recent years, Paul has shown no sign that he remembers anything from Rwanda any more. Repression, the counsellor calls it. Something about his young brain's inability to process the violence, apparently. I tell myself it is for the best. That if Paul forgets everything to do with Rwanda, it makes room for new, better memories, like feeding the ducks in the park with Agnès, or learning to ice-skate at the Hampton Court Palace Ice Rink at Christmas time, the two of us falling over into fits of giggles. That is my gift to him. A normal childhood.

For me, it is different. I left part of myself in Rwanda. Benjamin presents a tenuous chance to reconnect with my past. The past, *before*. It feels safe since he is under supervision and the charity will act as a post-box.

'If there is the slightest chance that my Benjamin is still there, I have to try,' I tell the counsellor, who greets my decision with magnanimous silence, careful not to interfere. She is only there to listen, she keeps telling me. A mute witness of the tug-of-war between the responsible adult raising a teenage boy as a single working mum in leafy London, and the terrified teenage girl still running in the woods, away from lake Kivu, haunted by the sound of crushed skulls. Time is meant to heal. All it does is to erase my other memories: Mama, swaying to dancing rhythms as she grates the cassava; Data, teaching me the name of constellations, sitting on our bench in the garden; Celine and I, inventing tales of forest giants to entertain my little brothers on the way to school. My little brother, Benjamin.

Paul has gone to the cinema with some friends from swimming club and won't be back for a few hours. I take the writing set I bought earlier that day from WH Smith from a drawer and place it on the kitchen table. The rectangular piece of paper is cream-coloured, decorated with autumn leaves. The set comes with matching envelopes. It feels important to have proper writing paper on which to set out all that I have tossed around in my mind for days. To find the right words. I take a deep breath, grab hold of a pen, and start writing.

> *Dear Benjamin,*
> *The volunteers from the charity tell me you*
> *have been in a rehabilitation centre for*
> *some time now. I read that the conditions*
> *in Rwandan prisons are atrocious. I'm glad*
> *you found a better fate. I hope this letter*
> *finds you safe. Much time has passed. I*
> *wanted to write to let you know that what*
> *happened was not your fault. I know that.*
> *You were only a child. We were all just*
> *children. Those evil men sought to take*
> *everything from us. I wanted to let you know*
> *that in the end, though, we overcame. Our*
> *past was stolen from us, brother. It is up to*
> *us what we do with the time ahead of us.*
> *Your loving sister, Victoria*

For a moment, I stare at the cream rectangle, recalling a little scrap of lined paper on which I wrote another message in a bottle, more than a decade ago. Better luck this time, I tell myself, folding the paper in half and sliding it into the matching envelope before licking and sealing it. I place it into my bag, then return to the sofa in the living room where I collapse, relieved. All afternoon I read, only getting up to make another cup of sweet chai.

In the evening, Paul returns, and we eat take-away pizza together. Whilst we eat, he regales me with a full review of the film he and his friends saw, an Argentinian horror film inspired by Guillermo Del Torro's *Pan's Labyrinth*. 'The director used the metaphor of a zombie plague to raise awareness of the drug problem in his community,' he tells me, his face serious. 'I read about it in a magazine.'

'So, it must be true,' I tease him with a smile, secretly impressed by his youthful enthusiasm.

'It… That's how Del Torro taught the American public about Francoist Spain… made them care, you know.'

I know, I think to myself. But what is the point in revisiting the past?

I smile at Paul. 'You recommend the film, then?'

Paul hesitates. 'Stop pulling my leg,' he finally replies, getting up to pour himself a large glass of lemonade.

Walking to work the next day, I notice the usual dog walkers carrying their morning coffee in compostable cups, dragging inquisitive canines away from their morning scents, eager to reach home before the rain breaks. I smile at the delivery man unloading crates of colourful vegetables in front of the little greengrocer, children in blazers and ties slaloming between piles of bananas from afar and homegrown Pembrokeshire strawberries, rushing past in an invisible race. Before I reach the school gate, a fine drizzle starts to coat my jacket. I try to brush the droplets away, losing my balance, and bump into a man leaving the playground, a copy of The Sun covering his balding head. A parent, I think.

He looks up, ready to apologise. When he sees me, his face contorts in disgust. 'Why don't you bloody go home,' he grumbles, accelerating his pace.

I have grown immune to such comments. They form part of the landscape in this part of the world. Parents see my skin, and they assume I am here to clean their children's school. They hear my accent and imperceptibly their speech slows as if I couldn't keep up. Today feels different though. Maybe because I wanted to scream back at the man that I no longer *have* a home. Maybe because his tone reminded me of another cry, in another school. Maybe because being back in contact with Benjamin only emphasises what we lost because of ignorance. I stand in the rain I no longer feel, eyes wide as the man walks away, the vehemence of his hatred insidious, familiar, like poison. Once he turns the corner, I hurry towards the redbrick building. As I approach, the sound of the school playground acts as a soothing balm. Entering, I move swiftly up the stairs to the classroom where pupils have started to assemble. As the ballet of dropped bags and dragged chairs plays out, I observe their young faces, wondering which of these children will inherit that man's irrational anger.

'Good morning, children,' I tell them, as silence falls onto the classroom. 'How many of you have heard of a country called Rwanda?'

Not a single hand is raised. No surprise there. Like so many things, Rwanda is not considered an important topic by the Department of Education.

'Have you heard of the word "genocide"?' I ask the class.

Some head movements. 'The Holocaust,' somebody says.

'But the Allies won,' another student says. 'They made sure nothing like that would ever happen again.'

'Yes,' I sigh. 'Sadly, other genocides have happened since.' And as I say it, I am suddenly compelled to tell those children about Rwanda, and Bosnia and all the other places where hatred prevailed.

'What are you talking about?'

I turn to the voice. The Head is at the door, attracted by the unaccustomed enthusiasm for discussion in the classroom. She calls me into the corridor, listens to my explanation, head tilted to one side, her empathy fighting her irritation. When I have finished talking, she pats my shoulder and suggests I take the rest of the day off.

'To rest,' she says with a conciliatory smile.

Deflated, I grab my jacket and bag, thank her for God knows what, and make my way onto the street. I walk aimlessly for several hours, wondering what just happened, angry at myself, at the Head, at the man in the street. Eventually, I reach a small park with a lake and find a bench. Two large swans bob along the water, diving into the dark green water, their triangular white tails and grey webbed feet pointing at the sky in a comical way, instinctively unafraid as if they knew they were protected by the Queen. For a long time, I watch these strange-looking animals, majestic, unaware of their entitlement. I feel sick. Spotting a large stone on the ground, I pick it up and throw it at the birds, meaning to kill. I miss. They barely register the ripple. I drop to my knees and sob.

It is dark by the time I make my way back to our flat above the launderette. I am welcomed by the flashing light of the answering machine. Three missed messages from the Head. I pick up the phone and ring her back. She answers on the first ring, as if she had been waiting by the phone. She speaks in rapid sentences, without stopping for breath. When she is finished, I thank her, unable to find anything else to say.

'Where have you been?' Paul asks, with the amused concern of a teenage boy afforded the opportunity to tell his older sister off. He shakes his head in a strange role reversal. 'Your Head called.'

I shrug. 'I need a bath,' I tell him, disappearing in the bathroom.

'Right,' I hear him say through the door. 'Who's going to make food?'

'You make it,' I say, my voice strained.

'Are you sure you're OK, Sis?'

'Tired. That's all.'

I take off my work clothes and drop them in a pile on the floor before immersing myself into the warmth of the bath. Through the door, I hear a clattering of pans coming from the kitchen.

'Food's ready!' Paul calls half an hour later.

I come out of the bathroom, wrapped in a fluffy cotton dressing gown. Paul has laid two plates on the kitchen table.

'Your table!' he announces, carrying a wooden spoon in one hand, a pan in the other, a tea towel thrown across his forearm like a fancy waiter. 'Have a seat, Ma'am.'

As I take my place, he serves the contents of the pan onto my plate, meaty white beans in thick tomato sauce.

'Voila!' He adds a slice of buttered bread to the side.

'Quite the chef,' I laugh.

'Baked beans on toast, Ma'am. They're just the best.'

'Thank you. We'll make a good husband out of you yet,' I say with a wink. 'Mama would be proud.'

He grumbles in reply, taking the seat opposite and diving into the wholesome plate of food.

After he has finished wiping the sauce with his bread, he looks up at me. 'So, are you going to tell me what happened to you today?'

'It's nothing,' I tell him.

'I'm no longer a baby, you know, Sis.'

'Fine. I... I lost it in school today. I told the kids about things... Some of the parents called the school...'

'What are you talking about?'

'I mean they don't want me at the school any more...'

'You lost your job?'

'No...Yes... I don't know.'

I explain that some parents didn't appreciate my choice of lessons and the school thought it would be best not to alienate them, particularly those who are governors.

'The Head offered to write me a reference,' I say.

'But it's completely unfair!' Paul shouts, standing up and hitting a cupboard door before walking out.

I hear the front door slam shut before realising that my hands are clasped around my elbows in a defensive posture.

The severance money from the school complements the money I have been saving, allowing me to purchase the launderette underneath our flat. I am now the proud owner of my own business: five industrial washing machines, two large driers and a small room from where I provide an iron and fold service. The launderette is open 24/7 and provides an Executive Service between the hours of 8am and 5pm, Monday to Friday. The job is repetitive yet rewarding, and now that Paul has gone to university, regulars provide me with a much-needed sense of belonging. Mrs Bale comes on a Monday. A small lady from Thailand who married a British cab driver, she brings towels from her beauty salon across the road to be boil-washed and folded. John D always comes on a Tuesday. A young man, he lives alone. I do his laundry and share simple recipes with him, so he doesn't starve since his girlfriend broke up with him. Wednesdays are normally quiet but on Thursdays a swarm of students occupy the launderette, bringing muddy sports kits to be washed. Fridays are the domain of mothers who meet up to share the week's gossip whilst school uniforms spin round in large drums.

In between customers, I read, I listen to the radio, I keep informed. A few days ago, the young President of France announced another inquiry into the role the Mitterrand administration played in what happened in Rwanda. One of many such inquiries that dredge up the mud of history, only to prevaricate about distended lines of accountability, long enough for this government to distance itself from that one. Sanitised once more, Monsieur President will play-act closure through apologies, delivered on behalf of lesser (ancient) men, for the sole benefit of his (young) electorate. Pretend guilt as political scorecard. At the same time, in Rwanda, the government of Paul Kagame has laboured to rewrite our history so that the people can get past their own guilt. The intention is good, but already I hear the signs of a witch-hunt, of history repeating itself. It is hard to know what is true from so far away.

Alone in the laundrette, I sit in front of the circular glass of one of the washing machines, watching water swooshing round into a whirlpool of colourful clothing. Bubbles form against the hard surface, instantly swept away by the next revolution of the drum. Purring, rocking the dirt away, until the clothes come out of their womb – warm, safe, unblemished. It is fitting. The machines don't take sides. They don't lie. They take all of our dirty laundry in and dissolve the stains away. Is it not all we can do? Months after my first letter, Benjamin has sent a reply, written on the back of my own paper.

He is well. Humbled by my message. After his trial, he was sent to a rehabilitation centre. A place to learn about right and wrong all over again. A bit like school, he says. It is a long journey back. With some help, he completed his studies. He is a history teacher now, volunteering at the centre. That is irony, or karma, or redemption maybe. He wants me to tell him about Paul.

Looking through the words on the page, I refuse to pretend. I want to find BenBen, my middle brother, as he used to be. But there are shadows, too. The ones we don't talk about as we continue to exchange letters – through the charity at first, then directly. I buy some airmail paper the colour of Rwanda's sky. The news comes with increased regularity. With each letter I feel a little closer to him, to our past, to myself. With each letter, keeping this secret is a little more untenable. I am scared. I write cautiously at first, choosing my words, editing what I share. Benjamin describes everything. His anger. His pain. His shame. The journey he followed after Paul and I escaped. He tells me that the sister returned for him. The wound had quickly festered in the heat; he was delirious. She got a surgeon to amputate the rest of his arm. All that is left is a stump.

> *For weeks, she prayed for me, Victoria. Fed me. Changed my bandages. She hid me from the Colonel's men. The Colonel who fled the camp when the men of the Rwandan Patriotic Front came. They took me into custody. I don't know why she helped me after all I did.*

I close my eyes, rocked by the whooshing of the washing machines, conjuring the gentle face of the sister. 'Because God loves all his children,' I hear her say. Compassion. Hope. Charity.

With the letters comes a realisation. Rwanda paid a heavy price, torn apart by anger. Our family too continues to suffer.

Reading about the way Benjamin turned his life around, I feel belittled. It is I who is living like a ghost, has done so for all these years, riddled with grief for those we left behind; Mama, Data, BenBen. I recognise my fear that someone would come through our door and take my little brother away. The Colonel's men, the police, an immigration officer, Benjamin. I have been unfair on him, on them both. I need to hope. On a whim, I send a reply.

> *Dear Benjamin,*
> *It is time. I have included a plane ticket to*
> *London. Please come back to your family.*
> *Your loving sister, Victoria.*

Closure is what the counsellor calls it. She congratulates me on moving past my own demons. She tells me I am finally free to live in the present. I feel like a small child worthy of a gold star. Still, she tells me, you have been misleading Paul.

'How are you going to approach the situation?' She asks.

Interesting choice of words.

'It's complicated,' I tell her. 'Paul was so young, and it isn't clear what he remembers.'

Paul has completed his degree and is back living with me. He has secured an internship in a marketing company near Holborn, has a girlfriend named Cassandra. Paul who doesn't know about Benjamin. Paul who looks so solid, yet feels so fragile to me. I remind her that he has never asked about Benjamin, or even about Mama and Data. As I say it, I feel absurd. She has been counselling him since we first arrived in London. She probably knows more about his state of mind than I do.

'It's important that you explain to him why you didn't mention your correspondence with Benjamin before,' she offers.

'He will be angry,' I reply, my heart sinking. Paul and I have been each other's family for so long. 'I fear he will see my silence as betrayal.'

'Have you asked yourself why you chose not to tell him about the letters, Victoria?'

'I don't know... I... Part of me hoped he had forgotten – about what Benjamin did, to Celine, to Mama...' My throat tightens, distorting the words.

'Did you fear Paul wouldn't be able to forgive?' She asks, her head titled to one side.

'I...maybe...that's part of it. I hoped he would forget it all.' I reach for the tall glass of water on the little coffee table by my seat, notice a tremor in my hand, take a long gulp to steady myself. The cool sensation numbs the fire in my throat. 'Have I made a mistake?'

'Oh, Victoria, no. There is no right or wrong here. Paul's condition when you first arrived in London was, shall we say, precarious. I mean, you were both traumatised. You were able to voice what you witnessed, but Paul... well, Paul was so young, he buried his feelings deep. It's not uncommon.'

'I did everything I could to give him a normal childhood,' I tell her, feeling defensive.

'You did, of course you did, Victoria. Nobody is questioning your dedication,' she replies, soothing. 'What I am trying to say is that there is no way of knowing how Paul will react when he's forced to confront this past he might not even be sure is real.'

There it is again, that knot in my stomach. I feel there is more she is not saying, bound as she is by rules of confidentiality.

After the session ends, I walk to Hyde Park and sit on a bench overlooking the Serpentine. It is a sunny day, and many Londoners have come out onto the lush green lawns for an impromptu picnic. Young professionals, picking at shop-bought sandwiches in cellophane, munching on crisps in little packets, sharing punnets of strawberries. I sigh, jealous of how carefree they are. I feel hollowed out. Despite all our years together, Paul and I have never revisited that last day in the camp. If we had, I would have told him that what he did, he did to defend me. My little brother saved my life. Maybe this silence was a mistake. I thought I was helping him, but maybe I should have asked. And now, here we are. No going back. Benjamin is due to arrive in three months, and Paul doesn't even know his brother is still alive. I drop my head into my hands, pressing at the temples as if I could squeeze out the right answer.

A loud burst of laughter startles me. I look up towards the group of young professionals. They are all standing awkwardly, shaking hands and embracing before returning to their office cubicles. I notice one of them, his face glowing the crimson red of cooked lobster in the midday sun. I check my watch. Time to head back. I stand, brushing the creases off my skirt. I catch a bus back to our neighbourhood, trotting the last few metres from the bus stop to the launderette. Inside, a customer acknowledges me with a nod. I hurry past him, aiming for the back room, feeling breathless.

Paul returns from work a few hours later. He finds me in the back, ironing a pile of shirts due for collection the next day. He weaves his way past bags of clean linen, dodges the rack on which I hang shirts waiting to be pressed, leans across the ironing board, and plants a kiss on my forehead.

'Evening, Sis,' he says cheerily.

'Well, you're in a good mood.'

At first, he stands opposite me, a strange look on his face. Then, stretching his arms in a comedic way, he announces: 'You are looking at the new Head of Marketing.' Pride floods his face.

Circling around the ironing, I grab him into my arms, patting his back.

'Oh, well done, Paul! You worked really hard for that.' I squeeze his tall, muscular frame, tears streaming down my cheeks. 'So proud. I am so proud,' I repeat, my head moving from side to side as if giving thanks to God.

I close the laundrette, pinning a sign to the metal shutter. *Unexpected closure, due to family celebration.*

We head back upstairs to get changed. Paul has booked a French restaurant. His girlfriend is meeting us there to celebrate. Looking at the handsome man standing in my kitchen, dressed in a perfectly tailored grey suit, I wonder what I have been so worried about. Paul is a man. A good man. What we experienced back in Rwanda is in the past.

Cassandra is standing outside the restaurant when the taxi drops us off, wrapped in an ultra-feminine summer jacket with large orange flowers selected to contrast with her elegant black dress and sensible flat pumps. The daughter of a Nigerian politician and a famous London artist, Cassandra is the kind of woman who holds her head high. She and Paul met at university. She works for a big fashion magazine, rubbing shoulders with established designers and ephemeral celebrities.

'Have you been waiting long?' Paul asks, leaning towards her with a kiss.

'Only a few minutes,' she replies, turning towards me to offer a smile. 'Victoria, how lovely to see you.'

Always so polite. I wonder what her family thinks of my launderette business.

Paul pulls open the door and ushers us through with a little bow. Inside, we are met by a short man with receding hairline dressed in a tailcoat.

'We have a reservation for three,' Paul bellows with the excitement of a toddler.

'Certainly, sir,' the man replies, his eyebrow imperceptibly raised.

He directs us to a round table by a window overlooking the passing traffic. As we take our places, he turns to leave. Cassandra raises her index finger lightly, her firm gaze on the man.

'A bottle of Mumm's if you please?' The man bows before retreating towards the bar to prepare our order.

She is in her element, unlike me; I have never been to such a place. I straighten my back in the chair, assuming what I hope is a respectable posture.

The waiter returns, carrying a bottle and three tall, thin, glasses on a round tray, perfectly balanced on his flat palm. He places the glasses in front of each of our plates, grabs the neck of the bottle with one hand, whilst tucking the tray under his arm with a sweeping gesture. He presents the bottle to Cassandra who gives her assent with a flutter of her eyelids. On cue, the man peels the foil, removes the cork and proceeds to pouring the bubbling yellow liquid into our flutes. I have only ever seen champagne on TV before.

Picking up her glass, Cassandra turns towards Paul with a smile. 'A toast?'

Paul and I lift our glasses in unison.

'To Paul,' Cassandra says.

'And to my beloved sister, without whom I wouldn't be where I am today,' Paul says.

I feel the flush in my cheeks. 'To your future,' I reply.

After dessert, Paul orders an espresso for Cassandra, and a liqueur for himself.

'Are you sure you don't want anything else, Victoria?' Paul asks in a tone that sounds contrived.

'You've never called me by my Christian name.' It unnerves me. 'What happened to Sis?'

Paul reaches for Cassandra's hand across the table.

'What's going on?' I ask.

'Sis, Cassandra and I have decided to move in together.' He pauses, scanning my face for a reaction. 'With the promotion and all, you know…' His voice trails off.

I feel stunned. My eyes move from Paul to Cassandra, back to Paul, hoping for any sign that I might have misheard.

'What Paul is trying to say,' Cassandra interjects, 'Is that we love each other very much and want to get married and start a family.'

'Yes, Sis. I mean, I can't stay with you forever. I'm twenty-five, I need my own place.' Paul sounds strangely defiant.

'And of course, you will be welcome any time,' Cassandra assures me, as if throwing crumbs.

I knew this day would come. But knowing and feeling are two very different things. Their eyes are on me now, expecting a response. Lost for words, I search the table for a cue. Finding only my drink, I raise the flute with a smile. 'To the happy couple.'

Paul's shoulders relax and I see his hand clasping Cassandra's a little tighter. 'You're the best, Sis.'

A month later, Paul and Cassandra move in together. For the four weeks in between, I barely see him. There are arrangements to be made, walls to be painted. His new job is taking him on the road several times a week. Cassandra suggests they hire someone to carry out the work, but Paul insists he can do it all. I try to feel happy for them. I *am* happy for them, genuinely. Yet every night, climbing the stairs to our little apartment above the launderette, I am filled with dread at the thought of the empty kitchen, empty of its chatting and laughter, filled with silence. The counsellor tells me I should be proud, that Paul's successful life is a testament to mine and Agnès' dedication. I reply that for the past two decades, I have been mother, sister, confidante. I have no life but Paul.

'You're still young, Victoria. Maybe now is the time to live your own life?' she says with a half-smile.

What does that look like, I wonder? Still, I have my own preparations to focus on. Benjamin is arriving a few weeks from now.

'Did you speak to Paul?' she asks.

It no longer feels appropriate. Paul has moved into an existence disconnected from everything that came before. How much can Cassandra possibly know? To mention Benjamin now seems irrelevant, cruel even. I did contemplate giving Paul a call, inviting him over for a chat, bringing Benjamin to meet him. In the end, I decided to keep BenBen to myself.

'Promise you will speak to Paul,' she urges.

I promise.

On the day, I wake at 5am to give the flat a deep clean. After-wards, I do my hair, slip into a dress bought especially for the occasion, apply some makeup. Agnès and I spoke on the phone the night before. She wanted to know how Paul was doing with his new life. 'And how are you feeling, Victoria?' she asked.

'Getting on with things, busy with the launderette, you know.' I don't mention Benjamin's impending arrival, even though Agnès knows we have been corresponding. She told me she approved of my ability to forgive.

'I'm afraid I have to go, Agnès. Can I ring you back next week?' I asked, keeping my voice even.

'Sure. It's good you're busy,' she replied. 'Are you sure you're OK?'

Agnès has always seen past my attempts at bravery.

'Positive. Next week then?'

I hung up and put the mobile – a present from Paul before he moved out – on silent.

'Heathrow airport, please.'

The cabby fiddles with a large GPS screen before emerging into traffic. From the back seat, all I can see is his head, not much higher than the steering wheel, shifting towards the screen every few seconds. The rest of his body is hidden, slouched into a car seat too big for him.

'Been in London long?' I ask, indicating the GPS.

'Few months,' he replies in broken English.

'Where're you from?'

'Kurdistan. Came for work. For the family,' he tells me.

I recognise the well-rehearsed bitesize snippets for the distracted bystander, but I have been reading the news.

'I understand,' I tell him. I ask about his family.

'Two sons,' he says, straightening up. 'You?'

'From Rwanda,' I reply, before I realise what I said. I know that isn't what he was asking. 'Came with my brother.'

'Wanda? Where's that then?'

I sigh, grating my teeth. 'Eastern Africa,' I whisper, then realise I wouldn't be able to place Kurdistan on a map either. We are both lone heroes of our own discrete narratives. That doesn't make us pals. I don't feel like chatting any more. Instead, I turn towards the buildings streaming past the car window. They seem lighter than I remember. Maybe they have been renovated.

'What terminal?' he asks as we near the airport.

'Terminal 5,' I tell him, checking the details on the yellow piece of paper I stuck to the inside of my bag.

A fifteen-hour flight from Kigali, two changes, three airlines. Benjamin might as well be coming from the moon.

The taxi comes to an abrupt halt. I pay the fee, thank the driver and venture into the giant airport, looking for an arrival screen. The flight is on time. I make my way towards the arrival gate, cursing myself for not bringing a sign. Will we recognise each other after twenty years? Then I remember Benjamin's amputated arm, and I shudder.

For decades I have held on to the image of a gangly boy in colourful shorts playing football in our garden.

'Victoria?'

The man in front of me is taller than I expected, already balding, dressed in a dark suit crumpled by hours of travel, one sleeve folded in half and pinned under his armpit. It makes him look lopsided. Forcing myself not to stare, my eyes travel towards the man's face. Deep crevices mark the space between his eyebrows, drawn into what I guess is a permanent scowl. His nose is straight, bigger than I remember. His lips are pressed into a strange pout. Shame. Or fear. I have been expecting remnants of the BenBen I knew, but it is Data's familiar gaze that stares back at me.

'Victoria?' he calls in a louder voice, taking a step towards me. 'Is that you?'

I try to move forward, but my knees falter. As I stumble, the familiar stranger grabs my elbow, pulling me towards him. 'Victoria,' he repeats, as if an incantation. '*Imana aguhe umugisha.*' He speaks softly, locking me into a one-armed embrace. God bless you.

'You look old, brother,' I say eventually, stroking his cheek before bursting into a deep belly laugh, tears simultaneously jerking from my eyes.

'We both look old,' he replies in an amused tone, his head cocked to one side the better to take me in, his brow unfurrowed. After a moment, he takes a step back and looks around. 'Where's Paul?' he asks.

Shifting my eyes away from his probing gaze, I gesture towards his bag on the floor.

'Shall I take this? Let's grab a taxi. We can talk when we get home.'

He follows without argument, pulling himself along with a strange shuffle, as if weighed by an invisible burden.

We pass successive information boards until we reach the taxi rank, taking our place on the passenger seat of a London cab wrapped in a colourful vinyl advert for some insurance company. The initial effusion spent, we sit side-by-side, awkwardly, the sudden proximity uncomfortable.

'Did you have a good trip?' I ask in an effort to break the heavy silence.

'Yes. I'm grateful to you for sending the ticket.'

I cringe internally. Try to redirect.

'So, a history teacher, then?'

'Yes, there's great demand for people in schools, to help reframe our broken history.'

I realise then that there is no room for small talk between us. He radiates a deep intensity despite his tired limbs, and I feel the urge to open the cab window to breathe some fresh air. I remember how cold it felt when I first got here, and stop myself.

'Are you cold?' I ask.

'It's OK,' he replies, pulling at his lapel.

Did I think this was going to be easy? As I search for something else to say, the cab pulls up in front of the launderette. Are we there already? The driver, an elderly man with rosacea and a strong Brummie accent collects his payment through the secure window as we exit the vehicle, speeding off as soon as our feet touch the pavement.

I make my way through the shop, not stopping to chat with the midday customers.

'This way.' I guide him through to the back, up the stairs and into the flat. As we step in, I brush the wall, find the switch and in the light of a single bulb, scan my place as if for the first time. I want him to be impressed. I march him around the flat, showing him the kitchen, the toilet, the bathroom.

'This is where you will be staying,' I say, opening the door to Paul's bedroom. 'You probably want a shower after such a long trip. Make yourself comfortable; I'll go and put the kettle on.'

He nods, dropping his bag onto the springy mattress. 'Thank you,' he says with a tentative smile.

I am glad of the empty kitchen. I fill the electric kettle with a wavering hand, flick the button and listen for the rising sound of bubbling water. As I do, I feel my knees wobble, forcing me to lean heavily against the countertop. My head is spinning. In the distance, I hear the sound of crushed skulls. Then another sound brings me back into the room: the combi boiler, firing up. He must be in the shower. Steadying myself on the back of the kitchen chair, I pause, then grab two cups from the cupboard and place them on the table, dropping a teabag into the pot. As I wait, the flowery teapot of that first day in the B&B flashes in front of my eyes, and the image of Paul scoffing a sugar cube.

'Can I do anything?' His voice startles me.

In the door frame is a man in pristine white shirt and beige trousers. Like a vision from the past, I am transported to Mama's kitchen. Data is standing there, wishing us a good day before

140

heading out to work. I blink, seeing the man's short sleeve sewn up to hide his stump.

'Benjamin. You look so much like our father,' I say, inviting him to take his seat at the table.

The rumble from the kettle has receded. I pick up the handle and pour simmering water onto the tea, under Benjamin's watchful eye.

'Milk and sugar?' I offer.

He shrugs.

'When in Rome, and all that…' I say, apologetic. 'Are you hungry? You must be hungry after such a long flight. Shall I make you something to eat?'

He grabs my hand. 'Come and sit with me, Victoria,' he says, drawing me towards the chair beside him.

There is no trace now of the self-effacing man I collected from the airport only a few hours ago. The intensity in his gaze unnerves me. When he next speaks, it is with the sternness of a teacher to a child.

'Tell me, Victoria. Tell me where Paul is,' he says, intensifying his grip on my hand.

'Don't you ever answer the phone, Sis?' Paul calls, barging through the door. 'I've been calling you since this morning.'

'Paul! Why don't you join us?' The voice of Benjamin rings in my ears. 'We're in the kitchen.'

'Who are you?' Paul asks, no doubt surprised by the familiarity of the man sitting in his chair. He turns to me with a knowing look. 'You didn't tell me you had a boyfriend, Sis.'

Paul moves towards us with the ease of someone familiar with his surroundings, one hand held forward to offer a cordial handshake. 'Paul, the better sibling,' he says with good humour.

Benjamin grabs the hand that is presented to him. 'Good to see you little brother,' he replies, shaking it firmly. Paul spots the folded sleeve, yanks his hand away, takes a step back. As he turns towards me, his face is contorted.

'What's this, Sis?' he shouts.

'Ah yes, it sounds like Victoria forgot to mention my arrival,' Benjamin replies impassively. 'Sit with us, little brother. Let's have a family reunion.'

Paul is staring at me now, his face a mixture of panic, confusion and anger. I show him the chair opposite. 'What's going on?' he asks, pulling the chair away from the table before taking a seat. 'What's *he* doing here?'

I press my lips together hard, eyes cast down, hands clasped together in a knot under the table. 'I…'

'What our sister is trying to say is that we have been corresponding for years, she and I,' Benjamin interrupts.

'What! Victoria… It can't be true,' Paul says, his voice breaking.

'I'm so sorry… I…' I try to speak but all that comes out are tears.

'Victoria tells me you forgot about me,' Benjamin says. 'Of course, I had something to remember you by.' He indicates his amputated arm.

Paul and I freeze, staring at each other now.

'Not to worry, kid. No hard feelings. In fact, I should thank you. The old wound allowed me to get *rehabilitated.*'

'Why are you here?' I ask Paul, finding my voice.

'It doesn't matter now,' he replies.

'I'm sorry. I tried to tell you. Somehow it was never the right time.' A pitiful excuse, my words wash over Paul's tortured face. 'I really wanted to believe he could be saved, that the BenBen of my childhood was still there, that we could be a family still.'

'See, this is good,' Benjamin interjects.

Paul's fists tighten at his side.

'Why are you doing this?' he screams.

'In the Centre, they taught us to face our crimes. To envision our victims' pain and make amends in whatever way we could.' Benjamin replies. 'I'm here to say sorry.'

A scraping noise interrupts him. Across the table, Paul has stood abruptly, knocking the chair to the ground. 'I've heard enough,' he says, crossing the few steps to the door without looking back.

A moment later, he is out.

'What have I done?' My voice betrays my quivering.

'He'll be back,' he replies hopefully.

I am not so sure. Rummaging in my handbag, I pull out the mobile phone Paul bought me and dial his number. Immediately it goes to voicemail. Scrolling the list of contacts, I find Cassandra's. It rings twice before Cassandra answers.

'Victoria! You've heard our news I take it?'

I'm surprised by her jovial tone. 'Hi Cassandra. Have you spoken to Paul?'

It is her turn to be taken aback. 'No, not since he set off for yours to tell you about the baby.'

'The baby?'

'I... did Paul not tell you? We're expecting. You're going to be an aunt. He was trying to get you on the phone, but you weren't answering so he drove to yours an hour ago. Oh, I hope nothing bad's happened to him,' she says.

'Yes...no... I mean, I'm sure he's fine.' I am unsure how much to tell her. 'Cassandra?'

'Yes.'

'Has Paul ever talked to you about our childhood?'

When I stop speaking, Cassandra is mute for a moment on the other end of the line.

'All I knew was that you were both orphans,' she murmurs eventually. 'I had no idea.'

We agree she will ring me as soon as Paul arrives back home. When I hang up, I hear Benjamin's shallow breathing behind me.

'I'm sorry,' he says. 'To hear you like that…'

Straightening, I turn to look at him. 'What are your intentions? Why did you come here?' I ask, my tone assertive, towering over his shrunken frame.

'I came to be reunited with my family,' he replies, contrite. 'I've been alone for all these years. I'm no good at talking to people any more. You and Paul had each other all this time.'

Watching him now, folded onto my kitchen chair, I recognise the boy from my childhood. BenBen. I move towards him, take his face between my hands like Mama used to do, burrowing deep into his eyes. There is no maliciousness in these eyes, I decide. Only the wounded soul of a damaged child. I hold him against me whilst he starts to cry, rocking him gently.

After Benjamin has gone to sleep, exhausted by the day, I go downstairs to the empty launderette and start on a pile of ironing for the next day. As I lose myself in the repetitive task, I think about what happened. Benjamin and I wrote to each other for years, sharing our thoughts, creating a new link where one had been broken. For Paul, the memories from 1994 are still raw – I can see that now. Benjamin is still the monster responsible for our mother's death. By assuming he had forgotten and shying away from talking to him about what he remembered, I didn't give Paul a chance to heal. I resolve to ring the counsellor in the morning, hoping she might be able to help. I realise she tried to warn me.

Before slipping into bed, I type a message to Cassandra. *Any news?*

Still nothing, she replies with a sad little yellow emoji. I reason that Paul has a lot to process. That he is probably out walking somewhere, clearing his thoughts. I tell myself he needs time, ignoring the knots churning in my tummy.

I am back in school in Rwanda, playing under the tree. I hear someone calling my name in the distance. I turn. Celine is standing halfway between the tree and our classroom, waving at me. She is calling my name. I wave back, gesturing her to join me under our tree. She starts running, but the more she runs the further away she seems to be, until Benjamin appears between us, his shirt soaked in blood. She is running with fear in her eyes now. I go to reach her, but she is too far away. I watch, powerless, as Benjamin strikes her to the ground. I call his name, willing him to stop. It is no longer Celine on the ground. It is Mama. And instead of Benjamin's boot, it is Data who raises his foot, landing a blow to Mama's head. I hear the sound of her crushed skull. I press my hands over my ears and scream.

I am still screaming when Benjamin rushes to my bed, enfolding me in his one arm. 'It's OK, Victoria. You just had a bad dream,' he reassures me.

'Mama,' I sob.

'I know. I'm sorry,' he replies, rubbing my shoulder.

How could I think this was going to be easy? I worked hard to create a stable base for us, normality. Look at us now, I think.

'Tell me about your dream,' Benjamin urges me.

'No,' I pull away from him. 'I can't.'

'You must,' he insists.

And so, I tell him about the dream, about the school, the tree, Celine, and him, Benjamin, in the military boots. I tell him about

Mama and about Data. He listens intently, nodding here and there. In the end, he takes my hand. 'I wasn't there when they executed Celine and the others,' he tells me. 'I was walking Paul home.'

He explains that the Colonel sent him home to deliver a message to our father.

'He gave me responsibilities amongst the Interahamwe, made me feel important. There was so much anger in me. Data always treated you like you were the special one. He never really saw me. The Colonel gave me a panga, a gun, men who followed my orders. He empowered me. That's what Hutu Power did, it played on young men's insecurity.' Benjamin hangs his head low. 'I realised too late that the Colonel's interest in me was purely precautionary. He knew Data had access to official documents that linked him directly to what was starting to happen. As long as I ran the streets with his men, he thought he could control him. But Data didn't come to the school. That's when the Colonel went to the house, to threaten Mama, because she was part Tutsi. What Data did after that…' Benjamin takes a deep breath.

'I know,' I say, bowing my head. 'I saw him again, before we left.' I tell him about the hut.

'As Kagame's army moved closer, the Colonel became more restless, more violent. He ordered us to speed up the cleaning process. We felt like gods, deciding who lived and who died.'

In my mind, I try to reconcile the memory of the gangly boy from my childhood, with the child-soldier armed with a bloody panga, the child-soldier who abandoned his own mother to die, with the soft-spoken man sitting in my kitchen. I clench my fists. 'Not gods,' I whisper. I fix his gaze and say, my voice louder: 'You, all of you, were possessed.'

'We were taught to hate,' Benjamin replies. 'You must remember what it was like?' he says in a plaintive voice.

This is not who we are. 'You made a choice. A terrible choice,' I tell him, refusing to make it easy.

'I did. And I paid the price,' he says, rubbing at his stump. 'Years in a Rwandan rehabilitation centre. I've had time to consider my actions.'

'Still,' I say. 'How could you hate so much? Your own mother…' My eyes start filling with tears.

'The Colonel said to get you and Paul. To take you to Goma. It was meant to be a trap. I thought Data would come back for her…'

I raise my hand to silence him, shaking my head violently side to side, 'No more,' I say. I close my eyes, searching for the image of Paul and Benjamin playing football in our garden, laughing. I inhale hard, trying to silence the maelstrom of emotions raging inside me. 'The past is the past,' I say finally. 'Now, we must focus on Paul.'

Benjamin places his open palm on my forearm, squeezing gently. Something passes between us, a tacit understanding that we will never speak of those days ever again.

'To family,' Benjamin says.

'To family.'

Twenty-four hours later, I receive a worried phone call from Cassandra. Paul never returned home, and work rang to ask if he was unwell. 'He had a project deadline today. They haven't seen him, and he didn't give them a ring.' Cassandra sounds frantic. 'This isn't like him, Victoria. Where could he be?'

I don't know. 'What about the guys from swimming?' I ask tentatively.

'I don't think so,' she replies. 'They haven't spoken in a long time.'

Now that I think of it, before Cassandra, Paul's life was split between his studies, his work, and the daily chores. I realise I don't know any of his friends now, not really. Earlier, I left a message with the counsellor. I ring back. The third time, she finally picks up. Hurriedly I summarise what happened. 'Did he get in touch?' I plead.

'Victoria, you know I'm bound by rules of confidentiality. Paul is a grown man. The best I could do if he got in touch would be to encourage him to give you or his girlfriend a call.'

I know she is right, but in my heart, Paul is a seven-year-old little boy with big innocent eyes. 'You have to help us,' I beg.

Benjamin pats my shoulder. 'It'll be fine,' he whispers.

But the knot in my stomach tightens. My little brother is wounded.

We wait another day, Benjamin and I sitting at the kitchen table, Cassandra by the phone. She notifies the missing persons unit, but the officer assigned to the case tells her there is little he can do. Paul is a grown man. Men do that, disappear, when there is a baby on the way. This is not who he is, I tell Cassandra.

In the flat, Benjamin and I hold on to a routine. I return to the launderette, focus on the pile of ironing that has accumulated on the counter, chat with the regulars, exchange recipes with the young man who lives alone. Benjamin spends part of the day visiting museums. Lots of history, he says, told from the point of view of the victor.

That evening, we share memories of a common past, forgotten flavours from Mama's kitchen. Paul and I had long adopted a British diet. Benjamin has bought plantain, beans, sweet potatoes, cassava, and turned them into platters of *isombe*, *matoke* and *ibihaza*.

'Who knew men could cook?' I tease him, thankful.

He reminds me he never married. 'A man has to eat, Vivi.'

'You're going to make a good woman happy one day, BenBen.'

He smiles at the nickname.

After the meal, he lifts me off my seat and twirls me around the kitchen to the sound of music coming from a little digital radio he brought along with him. The two of us laugh, moving our weary bones to the modern rhythms, singing along.

The ringtone of my mobile cuts through our gaiety. Cassandra's name appears on the flashing screen.

'Hello, Victoria? He's back!'

'Thank God. Can I talk to him? Where has he been?' I ask without pausing for breath.

'He isn't saying much,' she hesitates. 'I'm sorry Victoria, he won't come to the phone... I just wanted...'

I exhale hard, as if someone had kicked me in the sternum. Cassandra's voice fades to nothing and the warm phone burns my ear. My little brother won't talk to me.

In the kitchen, standing next to me, Benjamin has been scanning my face for clues. Seeing a change, he seizes my elbow, directing me to sit, and takes the phone from my hand, muttering words I don't hear into the receiver. I reach to take it from him.

'She hung up, Victoria. Cassandra hung up,' he tells me, as if speaking to a child.

'P...Paul...' I start.

'Paul is OK,' He tells me. 'The boy just needs time.'

Time. Is that not the mistake I made? To think *time* would heal him? 'It's late,' I say wearily.

'You go. I'll tidy up here.' Benjamin pockets his little radio.

I walk down the stairs to the sound of plates being stacked up in the sink. The clattering recedes, replaced by the familiar whooshing of industrial washing machines. I recognise the tremor of the high temperature cycle. The neon light reflected on the white tiles is hurting my eyes tonight. I close them, feeling the vibration of the machines rumbling through the floor. I perch on a low wooden bench customers use to fold their clothes, resting my back against one of the industrial driers. I am grateful for the feeling of metal against my shoulder blades. The familiar sounds from the launderette fill my head, shrouding a flow of regrets; the could-haves from lives interrupted, the should-haves from paths not taken, and Paul, the one shining light in the twilight of my existence, muted.

The crystalline ring of the launderette's doorbell forces my eyes open.

Iris

The glass-panelled door of the launderette chimed open. At first glance, the place looked empty despite the rumbling tumble driers operating in the absence of human supervision. Disappointed, I dumped the contents of my bag into the nearest machine, slotted a £1 coin into the powder dispenser and poured the soap directly into the drum, selecting the highest temperature. The engine got into gear, tossing and turning the clothes into a swell of bubbly water. I looked around for an indication of the length of the cycle, found none, noticed a message sellotaped to an iron shutter at the back, ink bleeding from the moisture in the air. I moved towards it. CLOSED DUE TO BEREAVEMENT.

Crestfallen, I turned on my heels and walked back towards my washing, staring at the clinically scrubbed floor tiles with a heavy frown. Was I too late? I rationalised that the owner could be attending a funeral. After all, someone must have written the sign. I imagined faceless shapes in black gowns surrounding a hole in the ground. In my mind, it was raining. It rained at my father's funeral. I was pulled out of my morbid daze by the distinctive click the machine emitted before coming to a halt. I pulled an armful of damp clothes out of the washer and carried them to one of the monstrous driers. When I looked back, the floor was smeared with my dirty footprints. I closed the door, pressed the worn rubberised button, and watched as the contents took on a life of their own, ricocheting from side to side like disembodied marionettes. I looked around once more. Still not a soul. Befuddled, I decided to return another day to speak to the author of the sign. Before I left, I looked for a mop to erase the dirty steps that smudged the otherwise immaculate white floor. I found none.

At home, Henry was busying himself in the kitchen, setting the breakfast bar for the morning, listening to an audiobook. He pulled his earphones out.

'Ophelia woke up whilst you were out. She asked for you,' he said in the cool passive-aggressive tone that he had started to adopt lately. 'Where have you been?'

'I told you I was taking the washing to the launderette,' I replied with a stubborn bite.

'What's wrong with our own machine, did you say?' His voice dripped with suspicion.

'The big machines work faster,' I said. 'You're the one who's been complaining about your shirts not being dry in the morning.'

I dumped the big blue Ikea bag onto the counter with an emphatic gesture that I hoped would end the exchange, and exited the kitchen. I climbed the stairs two by two, reached the bedroom and slammed the door shut. Inside, I grabbed my notebook and headed for the bathroom, the only room in the house with a lock on the door, and hid there, propped against the edge of the bath, until long after he had gone to bed.

Alone with my thoughts, I wrote frantically about the launderette, its proximity and layout, the disappointment at finding it empty, and the astronomical odds of finding the sixteen-year-old girl with whom I had corresponded half a lifetime ago, not only in London, but living only a few blocks away. It seemed unlikely – idiotic, wishful thinking on my part, but Sister Agnès had seemed so sure when I had met her in Paris.

I thought about fate. The invisible forces that wove a link between us all those years ago might have been the same forces which drove me to leave France, move to London, settle in this neighbourhood, become a journalist. Maybe I had always been looking for her. I felt frightened now. The possibility that Victoria could be so close merged with Sister Agnès' revelations. My father knew and refused to help. What must Victoria have thought of me? That I was a liar. After all, I had written to her that my parents would help. But they had told me they would. The kind of thing parents told children absent-mindedly, to appease them. Not so much a lie as a necessity. Every daughter believed her father to be invincible, yet the look of defeat on his face that day with the stamps had spoken another truth, even then. Victoria was a stranger. A child lost in a refugee camp amongst thousands like her. My father was working for the very ministry responsible for providing humanitarian help, at the heart of a coalition government butting heads with a President who supported genocidal policies, and his small group of initiates driven by obscure dreams of colonial supremacy. Nothing was ever black and white when it came to Africa.

Agnès had manipulated me to get to him, with the exalted naivety of the well-meaning zealot. A hero would have helped, maybe. My father was no hero. I was convinced he had carried that guilt to his grave, that it had contributed to him losing his mind, maybe. I could extrapolate all I wanted, but I could never know for sure.

It was dark by the time I unlocked the bathroom door and slipped into bed next to the father of my child. Pop psychology told magazine consumers that women looked for their father in a mate. I had married a lawyer. What did that say about me? A man who embodied a certain quest for the truth or a professional liar, depending who you asked. Suddenly, I felt a stranger in my own home. I needed to hold on to my family so as not to come adrift.

When I woke, it was to an empty bed. The square digital clock on the bedside table informed me it was seven thirty. Time to take Ophelia to school. I dressed hurriedly, rushed to her room, changed her into her school uniform, grabbed keys, mobile, notebook, and dropped them into my bag. It was seven forty-two by the time we closed the front door behind us, marching at a pace unsuited to her little legs, crossing two junctions. At seven forty-six, she went through the school gate and disappeared inside the red brick building.

'See you at three thirty,' I shouted after her.

As soon as I turned round, my phone rang. It was Kerstin asking for an update on my launderette visit.

'Nothing so far,' I told her. 'I'll go back in a few days.' I didn't mention the bereavement sign.

Skipping my morning coffee, I walked instead across London to Tate Modern, bought a ticket and went upstairs to the side corridor where I found what I had come for. *Untitled #97* by Cindy Sherman, a photograph I first saw exhibited in France representing the artist naked under a red bathrobe. The picture always spoke to me of objectification, of the violence men were capable of, and of our own vulnerability as women. Searching for Victoria, I had often thought of this picture. I thought of the tunnel in Paris where Princess Diana had died, chased by paparazzi, and of the debate it had sparked about journalism's loss of integrity. Looking at the picture today, I saw an air of defiance that had escaped me until now, the victim rising from under the oppressor's thumb, no longer content to be exhibited as fleeting entertainment.

As soon as the washing basket was full enough, I packed the unpleasant-smelling bundle into a bag and made my way back to the launderette. From a distance, I saw customers gesticulating inside. As I got closer, I realised the two women were laughing whilst loading and unloading bags of towels.

'Good afternoon,' I called, in tune with the door chime.

'Morning, lady,' one of the women replied, whilst the other welcomed me with a smile.

Throwing a glance towards the back, I saw the iron shutter was rolled up. Stopping mid-row, I emptied the contents of my bag into a machine, placed the dispensed soap in and set the machine to start. I folded my bag carefully and placed it gently on the little bench underneath the machine.

I had waited for this moment a long time. A sharp pain stabbed at my left shoulder blade, the place where I carried stress. I inhaled deeply and moved towards the little counter. The room at the back was deeper than I had expected from the size of the launderette.

At first, I couldn't see anyone in there. As I approached, I could hear humming, and the vaporous sound of a steam iron.

'Hello?' I called from the counter.

'Yeah, hello,' replied a baritone voice. 'Can I help you?'

A man with receding grey hair appeared in the window. 'Anything I can do?' he asked again with an engaging smile.

I blinked, trying to take him in. I noticed one of his sleeves was folded in half, secured with a safety pin.

'Victoria,' I said. 'Is Victoria here?'

I didn't know what else to say.

The smile on his face faded away, replaced by an air of deep sorrow. 'You don't know. I'm sorry,' he said, frowning. 'We buried her on Monday.'

'No,' I cried, dropping to the ground. Behind me, the two women had stopped laughing, alerted by the commotion. They rushed to my side.

'Are you OK, lady?' one of them asked.

The man lifted the counter and rushed towards me. Grabbing a plastic chair, he pulled it towards me. 'Here, sit on this,' he said whilst the women patted my back.

'Did you know her well?' the first woman asked in a soft voice.

'Yes, no. I mean, we hadn't spoken in over two decades…but we were friends once. At least I think we were.'

The two women looked at me with that forgiving look that said *you're not making any sense, lovey*. The man was scrutinising me with interest.

'Are you a relative?' I asked him.

'Benjamin. Victoria's brother.'

'Of course. There was another brother too, wasn't there?'

I caught a strange look between the two women.

'Paul. My little brother,' the man replied. 'Your accent. French?'

I nodded.

'Are you Iris?'

Surprised, I nodded again.

'You'd better come up,' he said, gesturing towards a little staircase leading from the back of the shop.

The two women helped me up and supported me to the bottom of the stairs in a silent vigil. Benjamin led the way up to a tidy little apartment built around a spacious kitchen area.

'Take a seat,' he said. 'Tea?'

'Please.'

I watched him busy himself around the kitchen, pulling mugs and tea bags from cupboards with his one hand, pouring milk from a glass bottle into a little pot, placing a bowl of sugar cubes in front of me.

'You'll have to excuse me,' he said, placing the mug in front of me. 'The teapot is broken.'

'No, it's great, thank you,' I replied, suddenly conscious of being a stranger trampling all over this man's grief. 'I'm so sorry for your loss.'

I waited a moment. 'Could you tell me what happened, Benjamin?'

The weary look on his face was back. He slumped onto another chair. 'It was all my fault,' he said, clenching his fist, his knuckles yellow to the bone.

I wanted to ask more but remained silent. He was clearly in pain.

'Why are you here?' he asked eventually.

How much to tell? 'I recently found out from Sister Agnès in Paris that Victoria lived in London. We are practically neighbours...' I feared his reaction.

'Ah yes, Agnès,' he replied with a sigh. 'She has been a puppeteer in our lives for a long time.'

I noticed resentment in Benjamin's voice, tried to change topic. 'How did you know who I was?'

'I found your letters in a metal box under her bed...You know... When I was tidying up.'

I felt ashamed to think Victoria had somehow kept our correspondence all these years, whilst I had lost mine. Tears started rolling down my cheeks.

'I'm sorry. We were kids.'

'It's OK,' he said. 'I never knew she wrote to you.'

For a moment, we sat side-by-side in silence. Eventually, Benjamin took a deep breath and closed his eyes.

'Victoria had a big heart,' he started. 'She brought our little brother Paul here so he would have a normal life. Raised him like her own child. She was a devout woman who believed everyone deserved a second chance... She found me when I was lost, wrote to me when I was alone, brought me here so we could be a family once more. There had been too many losses already, she said... When you've been to hell, you see, it scorches your soul. What we saw in Rwanda, what we were made to do, it's a lot to carry...I think she thought that because Paul was so young, he'd somehow forgotten. Then I came, and when he saw me...' Benjamin's voice faltered. He pointed at his missing arm. 'Maybe he thought I'd come for revenge... He ran off before Victoria had a chance to explain.'

'You don't have to go on,' I whispered.

'I... I was upstairs tidying the kitchen. Victoria had gone back downstairs to be alone. I didn't hear... I didn't hear until it was too late... Paul told his girlfriend he just wanted to confront our sister. Somehow, he got hold of her and started to shake her. As if he was possessed, he said later. Apparently, she fell onto the tiled floor and cracked open her skull. I heard Paul's scream, dropped the teapot I was drying, ran down the stairs, found her in a pool of her own blood, Paul collapsed by her side, screaming. When I approached, he yelled at me that I had done this, that it was all my fault.'

'It was an accident,' I said.

'Maybe.'

'And Paul?'

'The police came. By the time they arrived, he was incoherent. They've had him sectioned.'

Benjamin told me he made the arrangements for the funeral. A few customers came, as did Cassandra, pregnant with Paul's child. 'I didn't know about you until afterwards,' he added with a feeble smile. 'I found the letters, but there was no last name. I'm so sorry.'

'You couldn't have known,' I told him. 'I didn't know.'

Benjamin looked hollowed out, older than I knew him to be. 'I'll leave you now. I'm sorry I made you relive all this.'

'Please visit again,' he said as I got up to leave.

I realised he probably didn't know anyone else in London. 'Will you go back?'

'To Rwanda? I don't know. Maybe. Not yet.'

Before leaving, I scribbled on a piece of paper torn from my notebook. 'My number,' I told him.

Only when I got home did I realise I had left my washing in the launderette. It was almost time to collect Ophelia. I decided to return the next day. I ran all the way to school, found Ophelia, held her tight, squeezing her hand in mine all the way home. By the time Henry was home, I had prepared dinner which we ate together. I told him I found Victoria. That I was too late. Afterwards, I put Ophelia to bed, climbing next to her, wedging her in the fold of my arm, reading her a story. We fell asleep like that, wrapped around each other like wild animals.

The next day, and many days after that, I visited Benjamin. We talked. He told me about life in Rwanda. About his parents, school, then the radio station, about peer pressure and the anger of a lost generation of mostly illiterate children.

'Victoria was smart. She worked hard. I used to think she saw herself as better than us. It took me years to understand. She saw her education as the way to take care of us.'

Another day, he told me about Celine and about the many whose blood was on his hands. We talked about the Colonel. Afterwards, I did some research and found out that he was convicted of Crimes Against Humanity on the evidence Victoria's father had protected. I told this to Benjamin who replied that he didn't know where his father was buried, or his mother for that matter.

'Their ghosts haunt me,' he said.

'How did Paul and Victoria escape? Why didn't you?'

I told him I always imagined soldiers dressed in khaki coming to take the children.

'The camp was a bad place,' he said pensively. 'It corrupted our souls.'

'But not Victoria's,' I interjected.

'No. Not Victoria,' he acknowledged. 'She had her faith, and she had the sister. She told me she thought I was possessed. She never stopped believing I could be saved.'

After a while, I stopped bringing my notebook to those meetings. Benjamin and I took to arranging strolls around Hyde Park. He liked the neat garden, found it peaceful. We walked and we talked, him mostly. I listened to his pain, his grief, his regrets, the guilt that had corroded his existence, that continued to torment him. I showed him pictures of Ophelia, told him about my job. 'The strange thing is, I feel that I became a journalist because of Victoria. I always had it in me that I would find out what had become of her.'

He asked me why. I had been asking myself the same question for a long time. I explained about my father.

'I remember the French soldiers,' he told me. 'We were told not to fear them. That they were on our side. They let us operate in the camp as if we owned the place.'

'I could never find out for sure,' I said, averting my eyes.

'You were running from your own demons, then?'

I feared he wouldn't want to meet after that; instead, he told me that atonement was a powerful force. I looked at his ageing face creased by loss. It was hard to imagine this gentle man as a brutal murderer.

'I have many regrets,' he told me, 'but the one that brought me here was Paul. In our own ways, Victoria and I always saw Paul as pure, unsullied by what happened. Our redemption. I thought that if I could see Paul again, if we could be a family once more, then there was hope for us, for the people of Rwanda. I never imagined he could hold so much rage and pain that it would break his mind.'

'Will you go back?' I asked.

'Not yet,' he said.

'I'd like you to meet my family,' I told him. 'Will you come over for dinner?'

He smiled. 'I'd like that.'

When I got home that afternoon, I picked up the phone and rang Kerstin. She had been leaving me messages, asking for an update on the piece.

'Kerstin?'

'Ah, Iris. I was about to send a search party.' She sounded irritated.

'Yes, sorry. I've had a lot going on.'

'Any progress?'

'Sort of.'

'Do tell.'

'Well, I found the place, but unfortunately Victoria has passed away, so there goes my witness.'

'Surely there's still plenty you could write?'

'No, Kerstin. Sister Agnès was right. This isn't my story to tell.'

I heard a grumbling noise on the other end of the line. 'I'm sorry to let you down.'

'What happened to raising the profile of the genocide?' she told me.

'It's been a quarter of a century. People didn't show an interest then – what makes you think they would now?'

'But my readers, they would pay attention,' she replied, on the defensive.

'Maybe, in the time between their morning latte and the next commute – but then what?'

'I don't understand you, Iris. You were up for this. What's changed?'

'Nothing. I just realised I could never do the truth justice. I would only perpetuate a stereotype that's done a lot of damage already.'

'What about your career? Wasn't this going to be your big comeback?'

I knew this side of Kerstin all too well. She offered me more time, a bigger piece.

'No, you don't get it, Kerstin. I can't do this any more,' I snapped.

'Do what any more?' she replied, surprised.

'Write something that belongs to another. I can't. Goodbye Kerstin.'

I could have explained that I thought the truth would set me free, that what I found out challenged my preconceptions, that all I wanted now was to curl up with Ophelia and wrap her in cotton wool. Instead, I hung up.

At home that evening, I prepared lasagne. My father's favourite dish. At 6pm, the doorbell rung, and Henry let Benjamin in. The three of us sat in the lounge, drinking a cup of sweet tea, Ophelia on the carpet, drawing wonky towers with colourful pencils. At one point, she pulled herself up on the sofa next to Benjamin and pointed at his stump.

'Where did your hand go mister?'

Henry reached forward, apologetic, but Benjamin smiled in reassurance, and turned towards Ophelia.

'Once upon a time,' he started, 'a nasty white monster came to my country, poisoning people with enchanted words that spread a terrible disease which covered the land, driving people mad. One day, the poison contaminated my hand, and I started acting like a crazed man. But my little brother Paul, who was wise and brave, found a sword and chopped the poisoned hand off, saving the rest of me.'

'That's good,' Ophelia replied, returning to her drawing. After dinner, Benjamin thanked us and bade us goodnight. At the door, Ophelia handed him a drawing of a little knight fighting a huge dragon. 'That's your brother,' Ophelia told him, pointing at the knight.

'Yes, I think you're right, Ophelia. Thank you.'

The next day, he rang me. 'I've been meaning to ask you something, Iris,' he said.

'Of course.'

'Would you visit Victoria's grave with me?'

'I'd be honoured. Thank you, Benjamin.'

'Tomorrow, then?'

'Yes, tomorrow.'

The next day, I found Benjamin standing by the wrought-iron gates of the little cemetery, a tall woman by his side.

'This is Cassandra,' Benjamin introduced us. 'She wanted to meet you.'

'Lovely to meet you, Cassandra,' I said, shaking her hand vigorously. 'Benjamin's told me so much about you. Congratulations on the baby.'

We journeyed in silence along rows of carved gravestones surrounded by lush green grass, and the odd speckle of chrysanthemum, to a white stone. In the middle, a single word was engraved in gold letters. *Ubumwe*.

'Unity,' Benjamin translated.

Cassandra leant towards the vase embedded into the stone with a hand supporting her protruding belly, removed the dried-up flowers and placed a large bouquet of blooming sunflowers in its place, brushing the first autumn leaves off the well-tended grave.

'Look who this is,' Benjamin said out loud, bringing me closer.

For a moment, the three of us stood side by side, looking at the ground in front of us. Unity. I placed one hand in my pocket and retrieved a small envelope with blue lettering. I had written it the night before. 'For you, dear friend,' I whispered, placing the letter between the palm of my hand and the cold stone, feeling for Victoria's presence, tears streaming down my face. 'Forgive me. Forgive us all.'

'It's time to go now,' Cassandra said after a while, pulling me up, interlocking her arm with mine, so that when we walked out of the cemetery she felt like the dearest of friends.

'Let's go for a coffee,' she suggested.

Cassandra, Benjamin and I entered a little coffee shop with exposed brick walls, mismatched leather chairs and industrial lighting. We stood out amongst the morning hipsters; an ageing black man with a stump, a proud woman with a protruding belly and me, dishevelled, mascara blotched, eyelids swollen. The onlookers stared for a moment, then lost interest and returned to their computer screens.

We found a round table in an alcove at the back, ordered overpriced Kenyan coffee and gluten free, dairy free, vegan cakes which we ate in silence.

'Now what?' I asked, once our cups were empty.

Cassandra smiled and turned to Benjamin.

'It's time for me to return to Rwanda,' he said. 'I want to educate our next generation, so that our people learn to be one again.'

'What about here?' I asked. 'What about Paul, and the launderette?'

'Paul is finally receiving the help he needs, and when he comes out, we'll be there for him,' Cassandra said, rubbing her tummy.

Benjamin and I nodded in agreement. 'We'll be there for each other,' I said.

A year on, Cassandra had had the baby, a little girl she named after her auntie, Victoria. We had become firm friends and she came over two nights a week to share a meal with us. Henry helped Benjamin arrange the sale of the launderette and Victoria's little flat. With the money, Benjamin was able to return to Rwanda where he established an education centre dedicated to the next generation of Rwandans. Cassandra and I helped him set up a trust fund and the centre now provided ten scholarships a year to send promising young students to university. Benjamin continued to teach history. He had written a book about Rwanda's contemporary history, to help his students understand how the colonial influences had contributed to the breakdown of unity amongst Rwandans. What was intended as a textbook for a few had gained a lot of international attention, courtesy of Cassandra's family. Benjamin was regularly flown in to talk at conferences the length and breadth of the African continent. Wherever he was, Benjamin and I wrote regularly. I think we both felt it was a tradition that kept Victoria alive. In a way, we picked up where our previous correspondence had been interrupted.

Dear Benjamin,
Cassandra tells us Paul should be released
soon. When she last visited him, he admitted
he had no recollection of Rwanda, only the
camp in Zaïre. Cassandra wondered whether
you would know how we can best help him?

Dear Iris,
I enclose a letter for my brother. Please can
you make sure it finds its way to him. My
love to little Ophelia.

With the agreement of the doctor who treated Paul, I visited every Wednesday. I sat with him and read him letters from Benjamin. His older brother described their childhood in Rwanda: the house, Mama dancing in the kitchen, Data playing football with them both, Victoria planting flowers with Celine in the garden. Together they rebuilt a collective memory to heal Paul's broken mind. Paul had pinned pictures of the family home sent by Benjamin to his wall.

Cassandra arrived for dinner one day, little Victoria in a brightly coloured sling. Cassandra always carried her daughter close to her chest. Usually poised, she seemed very excited. I helped her unwrap the baby and we handed little Victoria to Ophelia who had become a very attentive sitter. She had lined up some stacking toys at the ready. Within minutes, the two girls were giggling at a rainbow of collapsing cups.

Cassandra followed me into the kitchen, where Henry handed her a drink.

'What news?' he asked, seeing her more upbeat than usual.

'The doctor called me in after today's visit,' she said. 'Paul's responding very well to the treatment. Benjamin's letters are helping enormously. He thinks Paul should be able to come out before too long.'

'That's excellent news,' Henry and I said in unison. On his own initiative, Henry represented Paul after Victoria's death. The court were told about his deep childhood trauma and agreed the death was a tragic yet unfortunate accident.

As we were about to sit down to dinner, the phone rang. Ophelia picked up. 'Seen any dragons lately?' I heard her ask. 'It's Uncle Benjamin,' she whispered, handing me the phone.

'Hello, Ben?'

'Hi Iris, I have some news. Is Cassandra with you?'

'Yes, we're all here. What is it?'

Benjamin announced that he had been contacted by a professor from Queen's College London. 'He's read my book; can you believe it? He wants me to deliver the keynote lecture at a conference in London in December,' he said.

'Oh, that's fantastic news!' I said before relaying the news to the others.

'Ask him if he'll be spending Christmas with us,' Cassandra mouthed.

'And what the conference is about,' Henry added.

'Global propaganda and the rise of nationalism in the era of social media,' Benjamin replied. 'And that's a yes to Christmas. Oh, and Iris?'

'Yes, Ben?'

'Will you come?' he asked.

'Sure, I'll be there. We'll all be there to hear you speak.'

Benjamin explained that Professor Melvern felt his book had what he called a worrying modern resonance in the West. 'With the perpetuation of fake news on social media, he wants me to tell his students about the role radio propaganda played in the genocide.'

'Well, that makes sense,' I said. 'There's definitely a rising climate of mistrust. Henry was telling me this morning that the BBC ran a story on how the country is split along educational tectonic lines on issues like Brexit.'

'He's concerned that people have forgotten their history, allowing politicians to play a dangerous dividing game,' Benjamin said. 'You more than anyone should understand what this means.'

Of course I did. We said our goodbyes.

After dinner, Henry drove Cassandra and Victoria home, whilst I put Ophelia to bed.   'Is uncle Ben OK, Mummy?'

I tried to explain in words she would understand.

'Are you scared of the dragons?' she asked when I was done talking, a serious look on her face.

'I guess I am, yes.'

'Did Victoria's daddy get hurt by the dragons? Is that why he's in hospital?'

'I suppose he did, sweetheart.'

Ophelia looked at the ceiling for a moment.

'Can Uncle Ben stop the dragons from hurting other people?'

'Not on his own, sweetheart, but he believes that the more people remember the dragons of the past, the more prepared they are to fight new ones.'

'That's very brave, isn't it?' she said, wrapping her arms around me.

I nodded.

'I love you, Mummy.'

On the day of the lecture, Cassandra, Henry and I took our seats on the front row of the large modern lecture theatre with colourful padded seats. It contrasted with the wood-panelled lecture theatres from my own university days, when the student population was as homogeneous as the walls.

The professor beckoned Benjamin to the lectern and introduced him. He stood straight, his one arm clutching his notes.

'In her memoir, the Rwandan author Clementine Wamariya wrote: "Rwandans believe we're comfortable with silence. But silence accommodates hate",' he started. 'When I was fourteen years old, I did despicable things because words like Hutu and Tutsi had been corrupted by those in power to dehumanise the victims and desensitise the international bystanders.' Benjamin described those hundred days from the perspective of the one wielding the panga, and the perspective of those whose lives he had cut short. 'When so many are guilty of atrocities, what can you do?' he asked. 'Do you encourage people to forget?'

'Maybe?' someone said tentatively.

'How do you educate people, then?' Benjamin asked the assembled crowd. 'How do you show those too young to remember how to prevent the perpetuation of divisive myths?' He went on to talk about the work of reconstruction, of the inherent risk in erasing the past, of the importance of promoting cohesion, of the need to educate the next generation to break those myths. 'In 1994, a million Tutsis and their sympathisers were exterminated over the course of 100 days because corrupt governments appropriated our history and created fake narratives to turn our people against each other,' he concluded. 'History is our greatest teacher. Unity our most precious legacy. This is true everywhere. Challenge those who tell you otherwise.'

That night in bed, Benjamin's words resonated in my head. My father loved history, but a man from his generation, raised as a war orphan in a military school, would have been taught a particular brand of history. A history of self-justification, of pride, of validation. The history of an industrial era when France was a great country, built on the successes of colonialism. *FranceAfrique*. A perception of the world through a prism that helped mislead not only the international community, but people of my generation too.

'Henry?' I said out loud in the darkness. 'I want to return to France.'

He sat up in bed, turned the light on. For hours, we talked about my father and all the unanswered questions that I had inherited when he died. 'I think I understand what I must do,' I told him.

The next day, we made a few phone calls. A week later, our house was on the market. A month on, after the Christmas and New Year holidays, we were driving down to a new apartment we had rented in Bordeaux. Henry found a lecturing post in the University of Bordeaux Montaigne, teaching International Law. I took a research post at the Institute of Political Studies where students destined for the French School of Administration received their training. I taught them about the damage caused by France's post-colonial policies, drew parallels with Michel Papon and the Holocaust, and explained to them that laundering the past only succeeded in creating a breeding ground for future atrocities. History, I told them, was destined to repeat itself unless we learnt from it. We talked about the rise of the National Front, about the climate of mistrust that made Brexit possible in the UK, about the people storming Capitol Hill in the US, about the 'them and us' mentality which dehumanised and created a mythical *other*. We compared the Rwandan radio of the 90s to the emergence of 'fake news'. Unity was under threat, I told them. Together, we could learn to recognise the signs.

Paul came out of hospital the following Christmas. Cassandra told me that his first visit was to Victoria's grave. She described the way he sat on the wet December grass, stroking the headstone with the flat of his hand, whispering his goodbyes, whilst Cassandra stood by his side, holding onto Victoria's little hand. Afterwards they took a taxi to the airport to join us in Kigali where Benjamin had invited us all to celebrate. We had arrived the week before and so Ophelia was the one who opened the door.

'Did you slay the dragon?' she asked Paul, her eyes burrowing intently into him. Paul smiled. In the kitchen, Benjamin was bending over a steaming pot, his back to the door.

'Welcome brother,' he said, his voice almost singing. Wiping his hand on a cloth, he turned to hug them both. 'Sit, sit, please. It has been a long journey.'

Paul nodded. Ophelia dragged Cassandra, Victoria and I into the garden. On the bench, she had lined up some seeds for Victoria and her to plant. Ophelia used a small shovel to dig the earth, whilst Cassandra and I guided Victoria's little hands to press the seeds into the ground. I wondered if the smell from the pan brought back memories for Paul. Through the door, I could see him looking around at what had once been his Mama's kitchen. Benjamin had said that very little had changed. The pan he was using was the same one Mama had once used to make cassava porridge. On the shelf, her little transistor still stood, gathering dust.

'This is where we spent most of our childhood,' Benjamin was telling Paul with a smile.

Back inside, I poured Cassandra a drink and, as Benjamin tended his cooking pot, we chatted about her parents, about the move to Bordeaux and how well Henry and Ophelia had adjusted to the change. I noticed Paul was sitting motionless, looking beyond the door. He stood and walked to the kitchen steps. Outside, Victoria and Ophelia had finished planting and were running after one another, giggling. I wondered if Paul remembered running in that same garden, playing ball with his father.

In the hospital in London, he had had time to excavate his memories, the ones from the camp at first, and then those from the first few years in London. Benjamin had written to him regularly, sharing his memories, the same memories he'd shared with me as our friendship grew, of football games in the garden, reminding him of the names of his school friends, of Data's fascination with the stars and Mama's all-encompassing love.

Benjamin walked towards Paul. 'Are you OK?' he asked.

'I think so.'

'This, little brother, this is who we are,' Benjamin said, squeezing Paul's shoulder with his one remaining hand.

After a few weeks, words in Kinyarwanda started to return. Paul told us he needed more time in Rwanda, to find his roots again.

'It will be good for Victoria too,' Cassandra said simply.

The three of them moved in with Benjamin. Paul found work with a British NGO funding work of remembrance to help the survivors overcome trauma, and to ensure future generations never forget. He helped create a number of videos to educate the young, and developed a programme encouraging families to talk about what happened in 1994.

After Benjamin delivered the lecture in London, he was invited to co-author a book about the responsibility of post-colonial nations in dehumanising native populations and its dangers. The book was translated into twenty languages with Cassandra's help.

After we returned to Bordeaux, Ophelia started writing letters to Victoria, telling her about life in France. She included the name of the friends she met at school and descriptions of the flowers in the public park where I took her to play. Cassandra read the letters to Little Victoria at bedtime. Victoria sent her drawings in colourful crayons of the flowers she and Ophelia had planted together.

Author's Note

What happened in those hundred days was misrepresented by the press and foreign institutions, painted as a spontaneous ethnic explosion, as if the events of Rwanda could not be helped. Almost three decades later, most people in the West have little awareness of what happened in Rwanda, and the international press continues to frame events in Rwanda in ethno-nationalist terms, writing about 'ethnic Hutu and Tutsi', perpetuating the lies which made it so easy to ignore and forget. I never forgot Victoria's letters, which I kept with me for many years, until they got lost in one move or another. I would often wonder what had happened to her and her family, whether they made it 'out'. Her ghost emerged at regular intervals in my writing, including once, maybe fifteen years ago, at a writing retreat where I met an NGO worker who had just returned from the region of the African Great Lakes, and offered to connect me with people who could help track Victoria down. She gave me a phone number on a little piece of paper and told me to ring when I felt ready.

The encounter had the texture of a turning point, a moment when you know the story is heading for a happy ending. Yet at the same time, I was forced to face the simple fact that Victoria's silence probably meant she had lost her life in the refugee camp of Goma, in the summer of 1994. I never rang the number, preferring to carry her memory intact, hoping she had lived on.

Then, in 2013, my father passed away, having spent the last ten years of his life pursued by silent demons. Born to a military family during the period of the French protectorate in Morocco, my father trained as a politician, an economist, and later an accountant, working in investment banking for a large portion of his professional life. By 1994 he had joined the civil service as Special Advisor attached to the Minister of Cooperation, Michel Roussin, as an economic expert, with responsibility for Africa[1]. It is only much later that the full implication of that fact dawned on me, my mind trying to make sense of fragments of memories from those days. By then, my father's mind had become unreliable. It was too late to ask any questions. Nevertheless, I was kept awake at night by questions about the involvement of France in the Rwandan genocide, and how this connected to the individual experience of my penfriend. As many authors, I turned to writing to find answers, pursuing these two lines of enquiry.

For months, I researched what happened in Rwanda. I found witness accounts recorded by NGOs; memoirs; recommendations from a myriad of commission reports; the extensive work of investigative journalist Linda Melvern, who successfully pieced together what happened from a multitude of sources, but also sought to find out why.

What we now know is that what the world press portrayed as a spontaneous tribal conflict was in fact the result of a carefully planned policy of fearmongering and dehumanisation going back sixty years; instigated by racist (and racialist) policies first introduced during the Belgian colonial rule, maintained by a nationalist Rwandan President, and facilitated by the sustained

---

1. In 1993, President François Mitterrand – a socialist who had been in power since I was a baby – was forced by unfavourable election results in the *Assemblée Nationale* (the French Parliament) to name Edouard Balladur – a centre right politician - as his Prime Minister, therefore creating a government of cohabitation.

military support provided by the French Government of President Mitterrand to the extremists in power throughout the 1990s; a support hard to comprehend alongside records of France's numerous attempts at encouraging a democratisation of Rwanda, through the Arusha Accords, and by acting as a broker in the region. Anglophone commentators like Linda Milvern hinted at misguided efforts to maintain a Francophone foothold in post-colonial East Africa, but it didn't seem to be sufficient to explain it all.

One thing that struck me when reading reports from diverse international sources, was the way accounts differed. 'Spontaneous tribal outburst', 'ethnic cleansing', 'complicity to commit genocide', 'mutual genocide'. Language – whether English or French – clearly framed different perspectives, illustrating narratives of self-justification. The more I read about the responsibility of the West, of the President of Rwanda himself, of the inaction of the institutions which had been created to prevent further genocides after the Second World War, the more I came to believe that I might never find satisfactory answers. Language failed Rwanda.

As a Franco-British author, the choice of English to write this story was an attempt to create a degree of objective distance from the facts, yet as I conducted more research, it became apparent that although part of the story could be based on recorded events, I could never do justice to the experience. All I could do was tell a single story.

I aimed to create a narrative fiction which could act as intellectual witnessing, hoping that through historical fiction, I could at least raise awareness of what too often feels like a forgotten genocide. Along the way, I was forced to question my own motives and legitimacy as the author. Through the character of Iris, part of the novel morphed into a reflection on intentions and legitimacy when portraying the experience of others. Casting a wide net, I looked at the portrayal of Rwanda in film, novel, and through graphic novels, and the response these had elicited. It became clear that although each could be construed as an act of remembrance, they could also be interpreted as acts of contrition, intended to provide what Giorgia Donà calls situated bystanders (those who neither took part nor acted against) with an opportunity for absolution and closure, glossing over the fate of the survivors, and treating them as secondary.

In writing *This Is Not Who We Are*, I was very mindful of this dichotomy. Whilst presenting Victoria's experience as first-person narrative, I sought to use the character of Iris, a French journalist and Victoria's childhood penfriend, to explore the moral implications of her using the story to further her career as a journalist; and her research to find out whether her own father, who worked for the French Government in 1994, had in fact played a role in the genocide. At the same time, I wanted the novel to move past the genocide, to put the survivors centre stage and explore the long-term impact on individuals and their families.

To fictionalise the experience of genocide in the context of the Holocaust has been recognised as a way to bear witness, and ensure learning is passed on from one generation to the next. To fictionalise the experience of genocide in the context of Rwanda potentially carries a different connotation, both in term of intentions (of the author) and of unexpected consequences (for the survivors).

Where the author of the work is not a direct witness who experienced the genocide first-hand, there is a risk that the work might be seen as a form of exploitation of historical events, of cultural appropriation, reminiscent of colonialism. This is particularly sensitive with Rwanda since there is a recognised link between the decisions made by the Belgian coloniser who artificially codified the distinction between Hutu and Tutsi and the subsequent political choices which led to the 1994 genocide.

Nyasha Mboti writes about the way Hollywood films depict Africa, taking the example of the film Hotel Rwanda, and the way it uses stereotypes to serve the Manichean view of the world which characterises Hollywood, criticising it as 'opportunistic recasting'. He writes: 'While the move to make Paul belong to one side – rather than structure his character in terms of a hybrid – helps drive the story of Hotel Rwanda forward by creating story appeal, the move is also, critically, a flawed one. Not only does it totalise Rwandans, but it reinforces a stereotype: either one is Hutu or they are Tutsi. In such a set-up, there can be no possibility of passage between the two. A stereotype, necessary for story ends, is, in this case, recast and re- formed.'

For Mboti, this type of recasting is ideologically selfish since it fails to show that moral categorisation is not straightforward when it comes to depicting the artisans of the genocide, or their victims. The over-simplification of Paul as the 'good guy' versus what Veld describes as 'the one-dimensionally brutal masses of Hutu perpetrators', coupled with the happy ending, denies the complex historical context, and negates the ongoing nature of the human tragedy, in favour of narrative closure.

In writing *This Is Not Who We Are*, I tried to avoid such stereotypes. Although we know that Victoria is Hutu, her mother and best friend are Tutsi, and we are reminded on several occasions that although her brother Benjamin participates in the killings, he is only a child. At one point, Sister Agnès tells Iris that it is not her story to tell, before we return to the voice of Victoria, narrating her life in the first person. Victoria can only show a partial (and imperfect) view of life in Rwanda, the genocide, life as a survivor. She is not there as archetype, but to tell her story.

Perversely, narrative closure also creates a temporal distance, presenting the genocide more as a moment in history then a reality which could happen again. In writing this novel, I was very clear that I wanted to focus on the ongoing experience of the survivors to show a more contemporary resonance.

In *This Is Not Who We Are*, Iris represents what Beer and Snyman refer to as an 'intellectual witness'. The events which follow the genocide are equally important, to show the continued non-existence of survivors to whom closure is denied. Narrative structure and perspective are intended to convey a sense of trauma to the reader, thus enabling the reader to bear witness. For Samuel, 'in order for the world community to gain some insight, albeit fragmentary, into the genocide, the trauma experienced by individuals in Rwanda needs to be conveyed. This insight is necessary not only to come to terms with "absence" and "silence", but in being able to recognise genocide in the future and re-forming a "never again"' resolve.'

Looking for lessons from the Holocaust, I came across Marita Grimwood, who studied the importance of capturing the ongoing trauma of subsequent generations, and of those indirectly affected. She showed that the use of different literary forms by those writers with no direct experience of the Holocaust provided opportunities to explore the Holocaust's 'ongoing effects in the present.'

The collective *Rwanda: Pour Un Dialogue Des Mémoires,* is such an attempt, offering a kaleidoscopic view from a group of students, historians, psychiatrists and artists who visited

Rwanda's mass graves, survivors and memorials. A second-hand account told by diverse voices. Testimonies, poems, narration, historical account, psychological analysis. Powerful. Shocking. It is telling that the collective was the brainchild of a group of Jewish students who felt a moral entitlement to frame Rwanda in the continuation of the Holocaust.

Rwanda is different from the Holocaust, however. Victims and perpetrators live alongside one another, encouraged to forgive through Gacaca – community tribunals. The truth is raw, shameful, divisive. The focus has been placed on re-unifying a people rather than nurturing a shared (traumatic) memory. It occurred to me that whereas there is an extensive canon of 'Holocaust fiction', written accounts of 1994 are either official documents, witness accounts or journalistic reports – accurate versions of the truth told for the purpose of justification or to apportion blame. Fictions are few, and often published abroad.

In working on *This Is Not Who We Are*, I was put in touch with survivors who kindly agreed to read the manuscript. I wanted to ensure that what I described echoed their own experience. I am eternally grateful for their generosity, patience, and encouragements. Through the magic of Zoom, we held conference calls at the heart of the pandemic, talking about their experience then and now. They talked about ongoing trauma, broken families, substance abuse. I asked them whether they felt resentful of my writing this book. They explained that in Rwanda the government has established a Commission with the purpose of vetoing anything written about 1994. More official truths. They told me that not enough is done to encourage families to break the silence and talk about the past with the younger generations. In her memoir, Clementine Wamariya wrote that

'Rwandans believe we're comfortable with silence. But silence accommodates hate.'

To me, the role of fiction is to give a voice to silence. The Victoria from my childhood is lost. My father dead. Fiction is all I have left to sound a warning bell. However flawed my attempt, I believe like Toni Morrison that 'from what I gather from those who have studied the history of genocide – its definition and application – there seems to be a pattern.' And I see this pattern repeating itself around the world today – words being weaponised to drive a wedge between people, populations being dehumanised through systematic governmental policies, (social) media being used to spread fear.

Recently, French President Olivier Macron commissioned a review of the role of France in the genocide of the Tutsi, lifting the fifty-year seal on the official archives. On 26 March 2021, the French Commission of Research on the Archives Relative to Rwanda and the Genocide of Tutsi presented its report. The document is 992 pages long. It addresses both the question of the role and engagement of France in Rwanda in the run-up to the genocide and of responsibilities that are political, institutional, and intellectual in nature, but also ethical, cognitive and moral. It explores the almost schizophrenic way with which the French Government thought to encourage the democratisation of Rwanda throughout the 1990s, whilst at the same time providing the extremist government with extensive military support in response to a mythical foreign threat coming from English-speaking Uganda and understood by France through an ethno-nationalist prism reminiscent of colonialism, projecting fears of losing a foothold on France's area of influence in Africa. The report states that 'this conception gradually spread through the ministries as well as the central administrations between 1990 and 1993, even if the analysis of the precise nature of the military threat posed by the RPF (Rwandan Patriotic Front) varied according to the services and the advisors. In October 1990, this threat was qualified as "Ugandan-Tutsi". This expression is frequent in the archives and reveals the French authorities' ethnicist interpretation of Rwanda. This conception persisted and fuelled a way of thinking where, given the Hutu majority, the possibility of the RPF victory was always equated with an anti-democratic takeover by an ethnic minority.

There seems to be no reference to the pogroms that took place in 1959 and saw refugee Tutsi forced out of Rwanda shortly after the country's independence from Belgium, who had engineered an ethnic interpretation of the terms Hutu and Tutsi, which historically referred to an economic status of land and cattle ownership.

Concerning the question of complicity in the genocide, the report concludes that there is no evidence in the archives. In terms of responsibility however, the report condemns the French Authority which 'demonstrated a continual blindness in their support for a racist, corrupt and violent regime, conceived originally as a model for a new French policy in Africa' – despite many warnings from neighbouring countries and even civil servants within the government, who were marginalised for their efforts. France failed to fight extremism and to encourage a policy of deracialisation; instead arming the extremist party militias who would go on to commit the genocide, until at least the government of cohabitation. About France's ethnicist reading of the situation in Rwanda, the report writes that 'this perspective corresponded poorly to the Rwandan reality given that the country's political and social resources were resistant to the influence of ethnicization.'

The report adds that 'ethical responsibilities regarding political action call into serious question the decisions made at the highest level that misunderstood events even when all the information was available', further adding that there is also a cognitive responsibility when a country fails to realise that its ethnicist reading 'repeats a colonial pattern'.

This 2021 report constitutes the most comprehensive history of France in Rwanda to date. The story that remains to be told is hidden between the gaps of memory, the omissions in the reports and the not-knowing what became of a single teenage girl with whom I exchanged letters for a few months in 1994.

Resources quoted in the author's notes

de Beer, Anna-Marie and Snyman, Elisabeth (2015) *Shadows of life, death and survival in the aftermath of the Rwandan genocide*, Tydskrif vir Letterkunde, Vol. 52, No 1, 113:130

Casali, Matteo, 2011, *99 Days*, Vertigo Crime, New York: DC Comics

Commission de Recherche sur les Archives Françaises relatives au Rwanda et au Génocide des Tutsi, 2021, *La France, le Rwanda et le génocide des Tutsi (1990-1994),* Paris: Armand Colin

Diop, Boubacar Boris, 2006, *Murambi, the Book of Bones*, Bloomington: Indiana University Press

Donà, Giorgia (2018) *'Situated Bystandership' During and After the Rwandan Genocide*, Journal of Genocide Research, 20:1, 1-19, DOI: 10.1080/14623528.2017.1376413George, Terry (Director), *Hotel Rwanda* (2004)

Grimwood, Marita, 2007, *Holocaust Literature of The Second Generation*, London: Palgrave

Lang, Jessica, 2017, *Textual Silence*, London: Rutgers University Press

Melvern, Linda, 2000, *A People Betrayed: The Role Of The West in Rwanda's Genocide*, London: Zed Books

Melvern, Linda, 2006, *Conspiracy to Murder: The Rwandan Genocide*, London: Verso

Mboti, Nyasha (2010) *To show the world as it is, or as it is not: the gaze of Hollywood films about Africa*, African Identities, 8:4, 317-332, DOI: 10.1080/14725843.2010.513240

Morrison, Toni, 2019, *Mouth Full of Blood*, London: Vintage

Norridge, Zoe (2019) *Photography, Film and Visibly Wounded Genocide Survivors in Rwanda*, Journal of Genocide Research, 21:1, 47-70, DOI: 10.1080/14623528.2018.1522818

Samuel, Karin (2010) *Bearing witness to trauma: narrative structure and perspective in Murambi, the book of bones*, African Identities, 8:4, 365-377, DOI:10.1080/14725843.2010.513248

Union des Etudiants Juifs de France, 2007, *Rwanda: Pour Un Dialogue Des Mémoires*, Paris: Albin Michel

T. Vambe, Maurice (2010) *Elements of the abject and the romantic in the novel Inyenzi: a story of love and genocide* (2007), African Identities, 8:4, 351-364, DOI:10.1080/14725843.2010.513244

in 't Veld, Laurike (2015) *Introducing the Rwandan Genocide from a distance: American noir and the animal metaphor in 99 Days*, Journal of Graphic Novels and Comics, 6:2, 138-153, DOI: 10.1080/21504857.2015.1027941

Wamariya, Clementine and Weil, Elizabeth, 2018, *The Girl Who Smiled Beads*, London: Windmill Book

Examining the past by accepting the factual truths is the only way to free oneself from trauma and its wounds. The teachings of history must not be fought. On the contrary, they allow for peace and remembrance, they give honour and dignity when the time comes for an awareness, for knowing the true reality of our world. This reality was that of a genocide, forcing the Tutsi into terror and destruction. They will never be forgotten.
Conclusion to the 2021 report *La France, Le Rwanda et Le Génocide des Tutsi*

Acknowledgments

The author wishes to express her profound thanks to the community of people who contributed to birthing this story.

To Mick, Sarah, Simon, Jamie and the wonderful people at Seren for their passion and expertise, and to editor extraordinaire Alison Layland.

To Matthew McKenzie, Sara Palacin Jones, Izzy Macfarlane, Jessica Shelley, Richard Gwyn and Richard Davies for reading early drafts, and especially to Jonathan Macho for his friendship and relentless support.

To Christian for his expertise of Kinyarwanda. To Claver Irakoze for his patience and wisdom, and for believing in the power of storytelling.